THE PROMISE

BARRIE WILLIAM BRYCE

*To Steven
May the Path you Walk
Be made up of
your Wishes
and Dreams.
Barrie William Bryce
20-8-08*

True Fiction Publications

First published 2002 by
True Fiction Publications
Garchrie Croft
Lochnaw
Stranraer
DG9 0RL

© True Fiction Publications

All rights reserved. No part of this publication may be reproduced, stored in a retrieval system, or transmitted, in any form or by any means, mechanical, photocopying, recording or otherwise, without the prior permission of the publisher.

ISBN 0-9542580-0-2

Printed by Juma, Sheffield

Chapter One.
Old Memories. And Loving Whispers.

It was Friday the 28th of September 1969, the time 9am, as was signified by the leaving of the early morning 30-seat single deck bus. Punctuality was never a problem, for Charlie Brown the conductor, he was a small framed man of five foot seven, with dark hair and pointed features. He had worked for the main line bus company for twenty-five years, ever since leaving school at the age of fourteen. He didn't know the meaning of the word late, he had pressed the conductors bell to inform the driver the passengers were all seated, and inform the passengers that the driver was ready to start the bus on its daily run to the nearest market town some three miles away. Today, was market day so the bus was full to overflowing with married ladies dressed in headscarves, most of which sat at least one small child on their lap. As they left the only main street of their farming and mining village, they headed down a steep hill known to every one as Yukkies Brow. The driver engaged second gear and left it there, the whine of the gearbox sounding out as it held back the weight of the bus with its overload of passengers. At the bottom of the hill, Yukkies Brow merged with the main road. The driver came to a halt at the mucky white dotted give way lines on the road in front of him, they were only give way lines so he didn't have to stop but the old bus was as slow as a box mangle and he didn't want some young whipper snapper to come flying around the corner in a souped up Austin mini and cause another accident report. If there was one car he and Charlie hated it was those Austin minis, they couldn't wait five minuets they always had to be in front, put two minis on the same road facing the same way and they both thought they were Stirling Moss. But today as most days in this quiet village, there wasn't another vehicle to be seen.

Looking both right and left, then right again just in case of a mini, the old bus turned left and headed for their market town destination to the sound of Charlie browns voice saying, come on ladies fares please.

The main road had been empty of vehicles, but if anyone had taken the time to notice and come up for a second breath from their deep in conversational pass time, they would have more than looked twice at the figure of the man who walked towards them on the pavement.

As he reached the place were the bus had turned left, he watched as it pulled slowly away. The whine of the gearbox getting less and less as the driver persuaded the old lass up through the gears. The only other noise to be heard was the sloshing of the bus wheels as they drove threw the cow pats left by Yukkies cows on their early morning walk, too and from the fields to be milked. As the man stood on the corner he seamed not sure weather to follow the bus, and he stood there talking to himself, looking first where the bus had come from and then where it had gone. Speaking in soft affectionate whispers he said. It'll be market day, today, wont it, don't fancy that. To busy, to busy, to many people. There was a quiet place up in the village and I have a friend there I would really like to see, stupid coming all this way and not saying hello, isn't it.

If talking to himself hadn't caused some attention then he himself would have, he looked like a tramp like person in his late forties, standing about five foot nine and weighing a trim ten and a half stone. His head was a mass of faded Shirley temple curls and he sported a full white beard, and apart from his black full length duffel coat and the haversack on his back, he looked like a wrong time of the year father Christmas.

Turning left up Yukkies brow he said in a voice no louder than a whisper. Thirty-odd years and the place still looks as I remember it, same quietness, same cow muck on the road, come to think of it, that looked like the same bus. With a stunted laugh at what he had just said he took in a deep breath, then sighed it out saying in a slightly louder whisper" of course you wouldn't know anything about those days, would you, I expect you will just have to take my word for it as always.

Yukkies Brow had been affectionately though unofficially given its nickname by the locals, they had called the Brow after the very mild and gentle Younghusband family who lived in a large bay windowed sandstone mansion, that stood impressively some distance beyond the tall sandstone walls that except for the impressive gateway in, ran the whole way up the right hand side of the Brow. On the other side, stood the much smaller tied cottages belonging to the farm workers, these were dotted in an un-regimented right hand curve all the way up to join the main street. As he walked up the hill, his strides were positive, there were no signs of the aches and pains you sometimes saw in a man of his age and what you would have expected in someone who lived rough and carried a haversack the size of a phone booth on his back. As he approached the Younghusband gateway, he came face to face with a large black and white horse pulling a milk float. Walking beside it, was Bobby Younghusband a small gentle man who looked more like a man of the cloth, than a farmer, his face had the look of a shy quiet man, his face was right.

The two men's eyes met and both men acknowledged with a nod as they passed each other. Bobby didn't look back at the stranger but he did raise his eyebrows and thought what a wild looking man he was, and he better lock up his bantams tonight. If he had looked behind himself he would have seen the stranger watching and admiring how the horse new every door to stop at, when to move on without being told and it did it all by watching Bobby.

The stranger also thought," he is still in the dark-ages, its 1969 and it looks like Bobby still wont give tractors the time of day. Still I suppose you can't blame him, he always did have a good way with animals and modernisation wasn't always best, though it's a pity he didn't recognise me

He turned and continued to the top of Yukkies Brow, were it levelled out and merged with the wide main street that had once been used in better times as a market place. Standing still, he let his eyes take in once more what had been memories for over three decades. To his right standing in its own walled gardens and ground was the ship inn, a very well kept establishment that still looked well used, on the front lawn stood a tall impressive hexagonal shaped flagpole that looked as though it had at one time in its life been a ships mast .The flag on the top hung limp in the still air but if the wind had opened it, it would have shown the picture of a three mast-ed clipper sailing on the rough high seas. A road divided the next building which surprisingly enough was a school used by all the local children up to the age of eleven, and seamed well attended if the sound of morning registration was to go by. On the far side of the school sat the villages second Inn and as the sign above the front door aptly pictified was called the swan. It didn't have the magnificence of the ship, being more part of a terraced row of houses but smallness didn't mean a lack of homeliness and cleanliness, the swan had all the womanly touches it needed and more. Terraced houses were the normal after the swan as far as the eye could see except for the one in the middle were a sunshade was being pulled out by a little white haired lady with the help of a hook on the end of a wooden pole. When Hilda Gibbons finally managed her task of keeping the morning sun off the home baked produce that lay in neat rows in her shop window she disappeared inside to the welcoming smells of shortbread, teacakes, meat and potato pies and if you brought your own cup or jug, her freebee to her customers buying any kind of meat pie was her gravy, made from a secret recipe handed down from her great, great grandmother. Even though Hilda had been standing a long way off, the stranger could see the changes that had taken place to this now smaller and frailer lady whose natural good looks thirty odd years previous could have dissolved the willpower of any man. But her shyness had kept her three steps in front of any man, and being unmarried and having no children gave Hilda a big problem. Who was she going to hand down her secret gravy recipe to?

    Without any wind and at over one hundred yards the smell of Hilda's" baking had reached the taste buds of the stranger, who without a thought, said. I know It Isn't your cup of tea, but my memory has been tasting that ladies cooking for years, but not of course the dead things, just those things without the dead things in. Hilda used to say to me what a good healthy appetite I had, but I definitely had high blood-pressure and should see a doctor, she didn't know it, but I had the biggest crush on her, and every time I went In her shop, which was more than I needed, I blushed like a beetroot, repeating himself, he said blushed like a beetroot, well that means my face went red. I suppose you are a bit young to know what it means, he paused for a second then said, I'll explain it all to you when you're older. His eyes followed the houses on the left hand side of the main street; they were worlds apart from the ones on the right. These were all detached with big gardens and out buildings full of nearly unused or in other words obsolete farm machinery. To his left ran I little tiny road that led to the farm workers allotments and to get to them you had to pass a little cottage with an extension, that was used as a sub post office. It stuck out like a sore thumb, looking nothing like the building it was attached to, but in those days nobody worried about things like that, the post office did a great job, it was part of village life and a foothold on the outside world.

Do you see that he said? Looking directly in front of himself, in the centre of what was really a nearly crossroads, stood an old but still working gas lamp about ten foot high. It in turn was standing on a six-foot wide one-foot high sandstone slab circle. What stories it could tell! I can remember seeing that little island, night after night, covered in men's bottoms waiting for which ever pub to open, and when they left the younger generation took their place, everyone in this village spends some part of their life there, I cant see them ever taking it away.

By now the stranger who talked to him self had been noticed, and more than he was speaking a few quiet words. He wasn't your every day villager, as could easily be seen. He had Probably escaped from the loony bin, or perhaps he was just an old man down on his luck. But what ever his problem they just gave him a bye, as from time to time some one of his sort would pass threw their village and scrounge a drink or a meal if he was lucky, then disappear into oblivion never to be seen again.

I think its time we went and met my friend, don't you? So turning right he headed down the little road that went between the school and the ship inn. He didn't have far to go, firstly passing a little chapel on the right where the Younghusband family took their worship not only on Sundays but also through the week. Bobbie's sister played the organ on most occasions he remembered. Next on the right was the reading room, he never knew why they called it that, no one ever read there that he knew of, as far as he could remember there was a full size billiard table in the front room and a little bit of gambling went on in the back room. Thirty years ago sixpence would get you a full hour on the billiard table before the light went out, that's if you had a sixpence to spend. In those days the old Riley table had seen better days, the green baize had worn through to the slate bed and the cues were lucky to have tips, maybe the management had got around to replacing the damage. He laughed to himself as he remembered the management, then, had put it off for ten years, so what difference did another thirty make. Things were always slow and mostly uncomplicated in these little villages and after two world wars that was just the way every one but the politicians wanted it to stay. The stranger wanted to check to see if his theory was right, but he had more important things on his mind.

As he passed the reading room, he spied the unused tennis court at the rear, the grass stood waist height and the centre net had all but disappeared with only the two outer net supports left standing. This is still a sad place; looks like the laughter never did come back.

Chapter Two.
Hello Old Friend.

His wandering mind came back to reality and to where he was heading, as a few more floating strides stood him in front of a pair of sandstone gateless pillars. What stood before him was the village and outlying area memorial gardens. Dedicated to the dead of two world wars, the size of a football pitch, its well-kept flower beds and grass didn't seem to have changed, it looked as if the same man was still taking care of its upkeep these many years on. The interior was surrounded on three sides by a three foot high sandstone wall, segregated every twenty feet by an eight foot high pillar some two foot square, on the pillars and walls where still to be seen the holes that once held the metal wrought iron railing that had been given up to be melted down for the war effort. There were two gateways, in and out, the one the stranger stood at, and the one on the far side. The rear was a plain eight foot high wall that bordered Younghusband land, and a curving meandering mature tree lined path that joined the two main gates was segregated in the middle with a sandstone wall engraved with the names of the dead of the previous wars. In the top right hand corner opposite the main gate, the stranger could see the green house and green painted wooden hut that the gardener used to cultivate his flowers and store his tools, everything was surrounded by a green painted neat little nee high picket fence, The whole place was one of tidiness, no litter, nothing out of place, if it needed painted it seemed to be getting it. Walking in through the gateway he followed the path to the smallest tree at the nearest end of a line of oaks sycamores and beech. The tree grew threw the well-cut lawn a good two strides from the path, dwarfed by its companions the little ash still looked strong and magnificent. Taking the two strides, he held out his arms and embraced its smooth circular trunk.

Hello old friend, he said as if expecting a reply, he then said oh I'm sorry was I squashing you, and moved his body back a few inches, still holding on to the tree he said its so good to see you once again.

HEY"YOU" shouted a tall thin man well past the age of retirement, the voice had come from the doorway of the green wooden hut but was getting increasingly closer, Cant you read, then his voice rose again OFF THE GRASS.

The stranger didn't jump or say a word, he simply lowered his arms and was about to step back, when his eyes noticed a small brass sign held on with a nail at each corner and overgrown in places with bark at the base of the tree. He sighed as he took in what he believed to be an abomination. Bending down he gripped what remained protruding of the sign with the finger tips of his left hand, and without effort, pulled it from the tree, saying in a strained voice, do they think you don't have any feelings.

The tall man behind, had been about to say more but found himself speechless at the ease and lack of effort it hadn't taken to draw the four three inch nails that had held the sign.

The stranger turned and looked up at the puzzlement in the tall mans face and giving him no time to bring forth the words that weren't available from his open mouth, shook his authority even more when he called him by name.

Good morning, Mr Brown.

You know me. Do I know you? We haven't met before, have we? Before he could ask anymore-unanswered questions the stranger broke in.

We met many years ago Sir. To be precise 31 years and 59 days, we were standing on this very spot, it was a very sad time. I held in my hand then, what I hold now, the only difference then, was the ash tree behind me had just been planted and this plaque was fixed to a wooden stake that was placed in the ground in front of her. Looking at the dedication on the plaque, the stranger shook his head slowly and said, for the young to ask about, what the old cannot forget. My friend was planted, in memory of what must have been one of the saddest times this village has known, not to carry the pain inflicted on her by these nails for the rest of her life; if you have some tar we can put it over the nail holes to keep any infection out, and of coarse another stake to hold the plaque.

Mr Brown had been an upright honest hard working man all his life, who had made and kept the gardens in the beautiful condition they where in, he had no reason to let any man talk down to him, but the words of the stranger made him feel ever so humble, he knew the man was being honest, he himself just hadn't looked at it from his point of view.

Mr Browns answer, came easy, saying, it shall be done, and continued by saying I remember that day like it was yesterday but I am sorry I don't remember you. As its coming up to my ten o clocks how about a cup of tea I have a primus stove in the hut and I don't know about you, but I need one, plus it will give us a chance to clear the air.

Leaving his haversack leaning against the hut wall the two men entered the green hut, were the stranger found it as clean and tidy as the outside. Mr Brown gave him the choice of seats, a wooden bench or a single folding chair with a cushion on that was obviously the one he used. Being diplomatic he chose the bench. Mr Brown pumped up the gas and lit it; once the flame had jumped around the circular burner he placed a tiny tin kettle with a whistle on the spout on top of the flames and asked what he took in his tea.

The reply was two sugars and one milk.

Mr Brown wasn't a man with a good sense of humour and simply asked, how do I pore one milk, is that just a small amount.

The stranger smiled to himself at the serious looking face and said, yes a small drop will do, thank you.

The whistle brought their attention to the kettles readiness and the boiling water was pored threw a tea strainer full to the top with dried tea leaves that sat on the top of the first mug, when the mug was three quarters full Mr Brown said, You can put your own sugar and milk in if you want, and handed the mug of steaming tea to the stranger.

Who still holding the plaque in his left hand said, Sorry where would you like this?

For a second Mr Brown went with the intention of handing him the cup to his right, but was taken aback when he realised the strangers right hand was missing.

Seeing the embarrassment on the reddening face of the man trying to give him the mug of tea, eased the situation by placing the plaque on the table and relieved him of the mug, saying. Its ok, its just an old war wound, I think everybody has one some were, unfortunately mine shows a little more than most, but lets be fair and don't let it bother you, it doesn't bother me. To be honest a lot of people have deeper wounds you cant see.

Mr Brown for all his age was still an intelligent man, who while giving a lot of thought to the words of his new friend watched the boiling water he was poring turn into tea.

He was still in deep thought as he sat down on his cushion, holding his black unsweetened mug of tea cupped in the palms of his hard skinned hard working hands, his eyes caught the strangers eyes glancing at the plaque on the table. And it hit him like a brick |(some people have deeper wounds you cannot see).

You came back to see the tree that was planted in the memory of the three little Clark girls.

It was the stranger's time to look embarrassed.

Well not exactly, lets say I was just in the neighbourhood and thought it too good an opportunity to miss.

Mr Browns curiosity was getting the better of him, but he was still a polite man, swallowing a sip of his tea to soften his dry throat, asked, would you mind if I asked you a few questions?

The reply was quick. Fire away.

I have seen a lot of things in my time some that defy belief. About six years ago in the national papers a young man came upon a road traffic accident were a lady was trapped under her car, and without any effort he lifted the car off her while someone else pulled her out. No one could understand how he did it; the car was twenty five times his own weight. The man himself said, he didn't know either, at the time it was shear panic and he must have had too much adrenalin flowing threw his veins.

Pausing for a second, with a puzzled expression on his face, he then said, there was no panic when you pulled the plaque from the tree; you did it as calmly as opening a bag of crisps. How did you do it, it must have taken more strength than that man who lifted that car, MUCH MORE.

The stranger smiled and looked up into the eyes of an honest man, desperate to know the truth, And said, there is no way I can explain what I did in mathematical, or even lay mans terms, Its simply mind over matter, I didn't want it there and neither did the tree, the tree helped me. I know that does not answer your question, but I think it's the closest I can get.

Mr Brown was not convinced, replying, being a church going man I would probably say you had a little help from up above.

Everybody believes in something Mr Brown, myself I have always found miracles a little short on the ground, If man has to believe in anything let him believe in himself, the man that believes in himself can do anything, perhaps the man who lifted the car did have help from upstairs but he will never find that out for certain until it is his time to be up there looking down.

Mr Brown was beginning to see how deep this stranger was, and said after some thought, do you think the three little Clark sisters are watching us now?

The stranger looked up from his still steaming mug, swallowed a sip of tea and said, Mr Brown the thought of them and the help the tree gave me, plus my own beliefs in myself was all the help I needed to remove this plaque, I know that wont answer your question and before you ask, I was one of the people who searched for the girls when they went missing and I might as well tell you it was I that found them and paid for the tree. That was why I was asked by their parents to attend the tree planting ceremony. And apart from the way I look today I was only eighteen years old at the time, that's why you don't recognise me.

But you recognised me the second you saw me, have I not changed just as much as you.

No, Mr Brown, you are a lucky man, apart from the wear

of the extra years you look just the same; you have probably had a very healthy life.

Mr Brown broke in, I have been lucky, and I love my fulltime, part time job. I should have retired two years ago but what would I do with my time and who would do my job, it takes a lot of effort keeping the gardens looking like they do. I only get paid part time wages, because the council can only afford part time wages. If I did retire who today would take my place, which person today would work full time for part time wages. I think the council will have to carry me out in a box.

The stranger smiled saying I'm sure the council will plant a tree in your memory, mind you, you look that healthy I'm betting that's a long way off. They should plant one now, you could care for it and watch it grow.

Both mugs of tea, finished, Mr Brown said I suppose I better get back to it, maybe even plant that tree. Standing up he collected the mugs and took them outside, washing them under the pressure of the one and only cold-water spigot that was fixed on the far side of the green hut.

Following in the other mans foot steps the stranger thanked Mr Brown for his kind hospitality, and picking up his large haversack, swung it up onto his right shoulder as though it weighed no more than a small bag of sugar.

Watching him, Mr Brown was again impressed. If you aren't pushed for time why don't you take the weight off your feet, take the seat by the sweet peas. And pointing in the general direction said, they are over there by the back wall, they get the sun all day there plus they give off a fantastic aroma this time of the year.

Taking his advice the stranger headed for the secluded seat, which suited him down to the ground, slipping his haversack once more from his shoulder, he lent it against the metal curled ends of the wooden railed bench seat, and smelling the aroma of the sweet peas. He said softly, as he sat down, is this not heaven, maybe not for you but listen to those bees it is for them, they love the taste of all the sweet things in this world. He lent back, and relaxing his body, he closed his eyes, and breathed deeply trying to take in all the glorious scents that Mr Browns memorial garden flowers produced, If I only had a nose like you he whispered softly and affectionately, the world would be so much more pleasant, but I suppose that is the down side of being a mere mortal. Deep in thought, the morning passed to fast.

Mr Brown worked away in the distance trimming the edges of the curving paths with a little half mooned hoe, there was no speed left in the ageing man but his dedication and skill had never left him.

The stranger had to admire the man whose life was in the evening of his three score years and ten. They were worlds apart in every way, but he couldn't help thinking the earth would lose a rare flower indeed when sundown finally came to Mr Brown.

Hearing a distant clock strike eleven. The stranger talked to himself again saying, I wonder if the food still tastes good in the swan inn, lets try it shall we. Raising himself up from the bench he threw the haversack up onto his shoulder and took in one last breath of the sweet air, and catching the eye of Mr Brown, they waved there goodbyes to one another.

The stranger tuned away and headed for the gate and the cross roads with the gas lamp. There was no one was sitting around its base, which proved the inns were open for refreshment, so turning right he headed for the front door of the swan inn.

Chapter Three.
No Room At The Inn.

The swan hadn't changed inside, as he walked through the door, the room opened up to his left and right with the bar facing him. Turning right he followed the varnished floorboards around to the left into what was an L shaped room, a newly lit coal fire smoked heavily up the chimney in the far right corner. All the original oak beams above the windows and doors stood proud of the plaster, with more oak beams running the full length of the ceiling. A table and two chairs sat in an alcove barely big enough to take them, and it was here he took his seat leaving his luggage under the table. The whole room sparkled with cleanliness just like Mr Browns gardens, only this had a more womanly touch and feel about it. At the bar stood two men, the nearer was a stocky built man about his own height, he had a square face and a broken nose that looked as though it had came in contact with something hard, possibly a building brick. He had natural jet-black hair, which suited his Elvis Presley hairstyle. There was nothing else different about him unless you counted the salmons tale that was peeping out the bottom of his three quarter length jacket, and a tiny red terrier no bigger than the smallest Yorkshire terrier perched on his shoulder like a parrot. The dog had coconut matting for hair and its perfect balance made it look as though it had been born there. The man standing to his right came right out of a comic book, he was at least six foot, wearing a Zorro hat and cape, he didn't look the cleanest of men with his very large unshaven chin and what under his hat looked like a nearly shaven head. In his right hand he was holding what looked like his very own, impatient, and empty pint mug. The Bar being empty, the only other people there were a three man light headed pop group who were noisily drinking, and setting up their equipment, in that order for the evening live entertainment, On an even noisier looking set of drums was written in big letters the impressive name JOE SEMPLE and the RENAGADES. All three men were in their late teens to early twenties .The lead singer Mr Joe Semple stood well over six foot, held up on a lightly muscled frame.

A ladies voice shouted from a room, behind the bar JOE SCATTER fetch that fish around here till I have a look at it, It better be fresh I don't want no spent fish in my house.

So the man with the broken nose had a name. Moving to his left he lifted the flap in the bar and disappeared to the room behind the bar.

The stranger in the alcove whispered we don't really look out of place here do we.

The same, but now even louder ladies voice was booming, five quid, for that, I'll give you four.

Peggy it weighs eighteen pounds exclaimed Joe in an exasperated voice.

So the lades voice also had a name, (Peggy), she must be the boss thought the stranger,

Peggy's voice boomed, Probably tasteless as well, I never did like big fish.

But it's a salmon Peggy, they all taste good, why do you think the Queen eats them, and all them posh folks. These salmon are the cream of fish. Think of the soup you can make with the leftovers.

Leftovers, Peggy s voice rose again, what leftovers.

The head and tail and fins and some of the puddings, our Mary makes great soup out of them. Joe's reply didn't go down too well.

Not in my house. I don't use gubbings like that, do you think we are still living in my great grandmothers time. Four quid and two pints of best bitter take it or leave it.

You are a hard women Peggy Bryan, I don't know how, your Tom, puts up with you.

Because, I tell him, he has to Peggy replied. A giggle came out of both of them at the same time.

Would you, throw in a couple of packets of crisps.

OK, but get out of my kitchen before I change my mind. Peggy, followed Joe, back into the bar, where she took out four pound notes from the till and handed them to the man who had now regained his position standing next to the man in the Zorro outfit who was still holding his empty pint mug.

Peggy took the battered pewter pint mug and without asking started to fill it with mild, the owners usual beverage.

She filled it to the voice of its owner saying, to the top, it only holds a pint.

Her reply was quick, having said it many times before. I believe you Skutcher, thousands wouldn't, and don't you ever wash this mug.

His reply was just as quick as Peggy s. Don't need to, it adds to the taste.

As the land lady pulled Joes pint of best bitter the stranger watched her closely, thinking her barks a lot worse than her bite.

Peggy was a large but not fat lady, the laughter lines, on her very pretty face gave her a permanent smile, she was probably a little older, than the stranger, but if she was, it didn't show. Peggy may some times, because of the job she did, had to act tough, but her real personality seemed to give out nothing but happiness and joviality, but that was just as long as you acted in a gentlemanly and friendly fashion towards her and her family.

Handing Joe his hard haggled pint, Peggy, glanced over, at the noisy evenings entertainment just as the front door opened. In walked, a leggy young lady dressed in what looked like a dark navy blue skirt that was really knee length trousers and a matching top. She had straight, shoulder length, dark brown hair and looked in her late twenties or early thirties.

Hi mum, she shouted at Peggy who seemed to beam with an even bigger smile at the entrance of her only daughter Margaret. In fact the stranger noticed that every one in the inn beamed a big smile and gave recognition at Margaret s arrival, she seemed to be a very well liked young lady.

Margaret lifted the flap and entered the bar, saying what do you need a hand with mum?

Peggy replied Joes got another best bitter coming on the house, and what ever you do, no more drink for the band, they had enough three pints each ago, I want them sober for tonight, apart from that everything is in the bag.

I see you have been doing a deal with Mum again Joe, I hate to think what it was this time;

Joe smiled and proudly said, Young Maggie It was a Queens delight I brought to the kitchens of the swan inn.

Oh, not one of those salmon. I would rather eat one out of a tin.

Joe a little hurt, made the mistake of speaking without thinking, saying a little to loud. Maybe it's the way your mother cooks them.

A big voice boomed back from the kitchens, There's nothing wrong with my cooking, have you suddenly got a death wish Joe Scatter.

She s off again young Maggie Joe said grinning and trying to talk under his breath.

My mums a mum in a million Joe and she reckons she s the boss because she's the biggest, and you cant argue with that can you. Now how about catching us a sea trout, they really do taste good.

Joe for all his extra years on Margaret worshiped the ground she walked on, so you could bet, a ferret chases rabbits, there would be a sea trout's tail sticking out from under that three quarter coat before the next sun rises.

The stranger got up and walked towards Margaret and the bar. Standing to Joe's left he asked Margaret In a quiet polite voice if the house put on early midday meals, but before she could answer her mothers voice came threw from the back.

We serve any time of day meals here.

Joe Turned to the stranger, and spoke in a very quiet voice, no more than a whisper, said, got ears like a bat that one.

And a face to match whispered the unshaven mouth of Scutcher.

Peggy's voice sounded back from the kitchen. I heard that. You got a death wish too.

Every one, except the stranger, closed their eyes. Opening his, Joe gave out a sigh and said see what I mean.

Looking at the woolly stranger, Margaret said, it looks like its your turn, what s your poison.

It will be if your mothers going to make it butted in Scutcher

every one was waiting for the voice of doom but it never happened.

You were lucky, Margaret said.

No I wasn't, I, just saw bat ears walk past the yard window and into the garden.

Sorry, Margaret said, just ignore them.

That's ok, good witty humour is hard to find nowadays.

Ye and getting blood off those varnished floor boards is even harder, not that I'm looking at any one in particular, as she stared at the man in the cape.

Could I please have a salad with a carrot and apple sliced matchstick fashion and a stone bottle of ginger beer.

The man in the cape spoke again. You must have been here before, taking no chances eh!

Smiling, the stranger continued, would there be any chance of a room for the night, preferably with a bath.

Margaret was pleased with her own quick thinking when she said, I'm sorry sir, we are full up due to the live entertainment but I will bring your meal over to you in about ten minuets, After I've served these two first.

The stranger had noticed the attention he was getting from Joes dog as it started to sniff the air around him, but a quick stare into the terrier's eyes from the strange seemed to changed its mind. As the little dog sat back down on Scatter's shoulder Margaret joined her mother in the kitchen with the order.

Looking twice at it, Peggy said, this is a strange order, a salad with a peeled apple and carrot sliced matchstick fashion.

Not as strange as the man that ordered it. He spoke nice enough, but he was a bit wild looking, To be honest mum I'm not sure I would want him around any longer than necessary. Never mind let him sleep in my bed. OH yes He asked if we had a room for the night with a bath, I told him no, we were full, well I wasn't telling lies was I, we really are full.

And you don't want him sleeping in your bed. You don't normally mind letting someone sleep in your bed when we are full, you know what its like in this job, we have to take it when its there.

I know mum but he looks like a tramp and he must smell, I saw Joes dog sniffing him, I didn't say anything because I didn't want to embarrass him. And even with a bath he might still smell.

OK love, you made your point, I'm sure it wont make any difference any way. . Mind you, he can't be much of a wild man if he eats salad, did you look to see if he has any teeth. Handing Margaret the tray of food, Peggy said quietly, try not to let him notice you sniffing him, when you hand him this or he might turn carnivorous and eat you instead of his strange salad.

OH mum, Margaret said blushing; you make me, feel awful.

Well I ask you Margaret; I know what's wrong with you, you've been watching to many movies, now get along before his salad gets cold.

Margaret collected a stone bottle of ginger beer and a glass as she passed threw the bar and placed it on the tray with the food and condiments, She found the stranger sitting patently in the alcove. Placing the tray on the table before him, said, I hope you enjoy it sir. And then excused her sniffing by explaining how she thought she was coming down with a cold.

The stranger surprised her by saying, I don't think so, your skin and eyes are to clear, but sometimes being nervous can cause a sniff. Margaret walked back to the bar, thinking, How close he was to the truth. At least she had skin and eyes; his face was covered in so much hair he looked like an old English sheep dog. Margaret looked at Joes tiny dog and thought, good job you didn't get any closer than sniffing, you don't know what you might have caught off him. Then turning her eyes to the stranger watched spell bound, as he started talking to himself in those little affectionate whispers. Worst of all he seamed to chew every mouthful at least forty eight times.

When her mother came and stood by her, Margaret said quietly, how long does it take to eat a salad, he has been at it twenty minuets and he is still only half way through.

Listen love, he's an old man, with probably no family, and if I am right, that would mean he has no were to go, so time will mean nothing to him but a burden, Give him half an hour of your time, an hour at the most, and I m betting he will be out of that door never to be seen or heard of again.

Ye mum, you're right, I don't know what's come over me, I should be ashamed of myself.

Well don't take it to heart, just be nice to him from now on; In fact, you will have to be, because I have just got to pop out to see Hilda for a second. Oh and remember while I'm gone. No more drink, for the band, I want them sober for tonight, and I can see their pints are about empty. Right, I'm off, won't be long.

Margaret wiped the spotless bar top and went off into a dream world of her own. It was a cosy life she had, there were always plenty of friendly people, sometimes to friendly. . Margaret had never found the right man. But her good looks and shapely legs and body, made every mans mouth water. Being in a public bar gave her much more attention than she ever really wanted. Her dream was broken to the other kind of attention she didn't like, a man who couldn't hold his beer.

Chapter Four Joe Semple

Joe Semple, the lead singer in the band, for all his drink intake, had overheard Peggy telling Margaret not to serve them any more beer. Now Joe was a big man, but he had no intention of trying to get around Peggy, when she said no, she meant no. But Margaret was a different kettle of fish, he was sure he could smooth her over with a little charm, In fact a lot of charm if necessary, because he was mister lady killer. So beaming a big smile as he walked up to the bar, and said in his most charming voice, three more pints for the band love.

Margaret smiled back, sorry young Joe, but mum says she wants the three of you sober for tonight, so I have my strict instructions, no more drink for the three of you.

OH come on love, one more drink won't do us no harm.

Sorry young Joe, mum said no and she says she is the boss because she is the biggest so I cant. I have my orders.

Joe was starting to get a little annoyed, and said, look love, we will have it drunk by the time she comes back, she'll never know.

Look young Joe, mum said no and I am not going against her, do you want to get me in trouble.

Even the drink didn't slow down his answer; I would love to, when and where.

Margaret came back just as quick, any more of that kind of talk and you're OUT.

Out were, Joe cried.

OUTSIDE, were else Margaret threw back, now if you know what's good for you, Go back to the band and sober up, OK.

Joe wasn't sure weather it was being refused drink, called young Joe or that his charm hadn't worked, but of one thing he was certain, he knew his manly pride had been hurt in front of his band, and who ever else was watching.

The older Joe could see, that the younger Joes temper was getting the better of him and said come on young feller, calm down, I'll see Peggy when she comes back in, and see if I can talk her into giving you'se a pint.

Shut up old man, you and your manalistick mutant of a village idiot can keep your noses out of my business; I'll serve my self, Joe said as his temper boiled over. Leaning over the bar top, Joe put his pint glass under the pump nozzle and started to push the pump leaver backwards to make the beer come out.

Margaret tried to force his hand from the pump leaver without success, and with tears of frustration running down her cheeks, she tried to take away the filling pint glass.

Were upon, Joe pushed her backwards with his left hand, with so much force she landed on her bum near the kitchen door.

Margaret s mum had just walked in the back door when she saw her daughter land on her bum in the kitchen doorway, hoping that nothing was hurt but her daughter's pride, she picked up the phone and dialled 999 saying its Peggy at the Swan we've got trouble, come quick.

Young Joe had half filled his pint when a tap on his left shoulder made him look around.

Chapter Five. The Quiet Stranger.

The young lady, said no more drink, I think she meant it.
The one man Joe hadn't expected to see was the old quiet tramp who sat in the alcove. Fearing no threat from this old man, Joe spouted off in a more than loud voice, Listen Jack Horner go back and sit in your corner before I put you there, PERMANENT.
The old mans soft face didn't look so soft anymore and the rest of his body didn't move an inch.
The singer snarled at the dogmatic stand the old man had made in front of him, and with suicidal force threw a punch at the strangers face.
The old mans speed was phenomenal, his left arm came up and deflected the blow, to his left, and in one continues movement his own fist shot forward, but instead of hitting Joe square in his wide open face he grabbed the singers nose between his thumb and fore finger, pinching it hard, with a twist thrown in for good measure.
Joes shriek of pain was heard and felt by every one in the Inn. And although there wasn't one person who didn't think he didn't deserved what he was getting, both members of the band still came to his rescue, or tried to. Dodging the stools and tables, and not showing any signs of the affects of being drunk the second member of the band charged like a man possessed. He didn't look as though he knew what he was going to do when he got there; He just wanted to get there. As he reached the stranger he was Screaming let go of him or I will. ERRR ERR those where all the words he got out.
Without moving his body or leaving go of his prize possession, That being Joes nose, the stranger let fly a kick with his right, foot, which caught the oncoming teenager low in the chest, taking the wind and any heart right out of him, As he

crumpled to the varnished floor boards, holding with both hands the place were the strangers foot had connected, he was trying his best to groan and gasp for breath at the same time. The two men looked down on him, but only one spoke, the one that put him there. Don't try to get up, stay were you are and try to breath short shallow fast breaths of air, it's the only way to get the oxygen back into your lungs quickly and take away the pain, of coarse you wont have any extra pain if you stay calm when the first lot of pain goes away. The stranger said no more, as he looked up he saw the remaining band member pick up a stool and slowly walk forward. When the stranger spoke again, his voice was fair, calm, and straight to the point, leaving no doubt in any ones mind that he meant every word he said. So you think you are old enough to be a man, well I'll tell you Son, you can wear that stool for a collar, or you can sit on it, what's it to be?

The witty Zorro s whiskery face held a grin from ear to ear; it made his enormous unshaven chin look even enormous-err. Shaking his head slowly from side to side, he looked down on the shoulder length blond hair of the trembling youths head. Saying, young feller, I don't think you would suit the colour, so if I were you, I would take, the man's advice and use the stool for what it was intended.

Everyone including the stranger looked at Zorro, it was strange to here him talk like that, he almost sounded educated. But educated or not, the teenager took his advice, not that he hadn't already intended doing so because he had.

Margaret picked her self up and walking back to the bar dusted the none existent dust from the seat of her knee length trousers. She was about to give the band their marching orders, when the stranger exchanged young Joes nose for a nerve hold grip on his neck, revealing a large round blood blister, the size of a sixpence right on the end of his nose, this put a smile on everyone's face

Reading the expression on Margaret's face, the stranger said, in his same quiet voice, it would be a shame to spoil a good night, when so much work has already been done. Then catching sight of the blood blister on the end of young Joes nose said, I suggest that you, Rudolf, say sorry to the young lady and then Both you and your two friends, Donner and Blitzen buy the house a round of drinks. That's of coarse if the young lady agrees, and then we can call it a day.

Margaret could see that the old mans reasoning made sense, and added I'll agree, but young Joe you better grovel, and I mean grovel.

I'm sorry Margaret, I really am, I'm stupid, that's what I am, Tell you what, If I pay for the drinks and we play an hour extra time for free will you not tell your mum.

A loud voice came from the kitchen. Her mum already knows, so You will play two hours extra Joe Semple and that will make up for me having to explain to the police when they get here that everything is OK. OK.

A very small meek and mild voice came back from the large young man. Yes of coarse misses Bryan, what ever you say.

Ye well we were all young once, put in the stranger. Then added, sometimes we have to learn the hard way, but it's not fair to learn at other peoples expense, catch my drift.

Joe nodded, and then said to his mates, come on before we learn anything else the hard way.

The newly educated voice spoke up, For some of us, being young once was a long time ago, and its getting further away by the second and talking about expense, if everything is hunky dory and he's paying, put me a whisky a brandy and a rum in me pint mug.

Joe Semple put his hand in his trouser pocket and felt around. Looking up at Peggy he said sheepishly, would it be ok to take the drink money out of our wages, I must have ran out. The stranger felt sorry at Joe's embarrassment, as Peggy shook her head in disbelief and agreement, then turned to serve the freebies.

Returning to his table the stranger picked up the tray holding his empty plate and returned it to the bar.

Peggy came over and said the salad ok, I think your meal

should come out of Young Joes wages as well don't you.

He replied with a little smile on his face I think he has learned his lesson and we don't need to rub it in, he isn't going to forget today for a long time, if ever.

Yes I suppose your right, so how about we just say it's on the house for all the help and the trouble you saved us.

Still smiling, the stranger looked up at Peggy and said thanks but no thanks, times are hard and they don't seem to be getting better, we all have to take what we can when we can and your needs are a lot greater than ours. If the salad had been bad I would have told you so, and then I wouldn't have paid for it, but as it was good and just as I requested, then it couldn't be better than that could it. Mind you the floorshow was a bit much.

Having paid for the salad his eyes left hers and she thought to herself as she watched him pick up his haversack and walk out the door, he has the most painful saddest eyes I have ever seen, what ever is hurting him, no amount of hair or smiles will ever hide.

A second set of eyes watched the door closing, and with her conscience stabbing her in the heart Margaret looked to her mother for help.

Reading the look on her daughters face, she said with some urgency, if you have changed your mind, do something about it; you are old enough to make up your own mind now. Whatever you say love; you know it will be fine with me.

Margaret left the bar and followed the stranger's footsteps out of the front door and onto the main street. Looking first to the right and then to the left she found her quarry had already disappeared out of sight.

Crossing the street towards her carrying a small nine rung pointy topped wooden ladder and an empty metal bucket with a chammy leather inside, was Father Eric Holm the weekly window cleaner. Eric was known as Father Eric because of having a son of the same name who wouldn't be called junior.

Margaret asked in a panicking voice, Father Eric, have

you seen a tramp in a long black coat, he just left the inn a few minutes ago.

Ye I did, he was talking to himself; mind you I couldn't hear what he was saying, not that I was listening, odd sort of feller.

Yes that was him Father Eric. Did you see which way he went?

Hearing the panic in her voice, Eric said, has he stolen something?

No, nothing like that, in fact totally the opposite, I've just got to find him.

He went around the corner down to the memorial gardens. The words had barely left Father Eric's lips as he watched Margaret rush past him and turn left after the school. Placing the pointed end of the ladder on the window sill of the inns end bedroom window he couldn't help saying to himself, by has she got good legs. Then thinking it must be catching, said to himself, I'm talking to myself now. Leaving his ladder, Father Eric opened the Swans front door and shouted as he entered, any chance of some hot water Peggy love for the windows, and carried on by saying with a dream on his face, ay Peggy just think if I wasn't happily married to our lass I could be your son in law.

Passing the bucket under the bar flap to Peggy, she replied as she took it into the kitchen to fill. You are forgetting a few things Eric, like the twenty years difference in age and possibly me putting cold water in this bucket and poring it over your head.

Eric went and stood next to fisherman Joe and to be honest except for Eric being slightly shorter by about two inches they could have been brothers, right down to the broken nose and the Elvis hair cut. Looking at Joe Eric said can't a man dream.

Not about my daughter came back Peggy's voice from the kitchen.

Ears like a bat Zorro butted in.

The voice came back again. Thin ice, that's what your on Scutcher.

The three of them smiled to each other as Peggy came back with the steaming bucket of not water and placed it gently on the floor under the bar flap.

Drink Eric, while the waters cooling.

Go on then, you twisted my arm, give us a half, no sense in me falling of my ladder, anyway how come you never give me water I can use right away? I always end up spending more than I get off you.

Peggy never answered but thought to her self that's what I call good business.

Chapter Six.
The Great Hayborough, Post Office Robbery.

Margaret caught up with the stranger as he was passing the memorial gardens; it looked to her as though he was simply moving on out of her village maybe forever. Wait she cried out, listen I'm so sorry, I made a big mistake, we do have a room for the night with the use of a bath, that's of coarse if you still want to stay.

He Waited until the puffing Margaret regained her wind and composure and politely said, that would be very nice, it's been a long time since we have spent a night not under the stars, not that we mind its very enjoyable, though September nights can be long, cold and noisy. Mind you I suppose that's all part of the fun, to hear all the night noises proves the world is still alive and us with it.

Margaret started doubting whether she had done the right thing, this old man was well mixed up, possibly away with the fairies and she started wondering if he would have the money to pay. Then her guilty conscience kicked in again, thinking out aloud she said its ok if you don't have the money I'll pay, it's the least I can do.

The stranger smiled, and said, its true I'm a rich man in a lot of things, though money isn't one of them, I do have enough for my every day needs and that includes staying at the swan. But I will still have to call in at the post office to get a little extra money to tide me over, I take it the post office is still open to the public.

Oh yes we use it every day to bank our takings, in fact my dads a post man that's how mum and dad met they were both in the post office at the same time, the post office never closes here not even for dinner time. Mister Blacklock says it's a waste to close when people want to spend money; he's a bit like my mum come to think of it.

Walking side by side they headed back towards the main street, looking like the most oddest couple of all time, they resembled beauty and the beast without a doubt.

Margaret asked him why had he come to her village and did he have relatives in the area.

His answers were easy, he hadn't come to her village for anything, he was just passing through and as for relatives his only one was an adopted tree.

Margaret thought, this man talks and acts so gentle yet he was so good when it came to violence, if he had an adopted tree as a relative and believed it, he must live in a world of his own. Margaret didn't have the worldly knowledge her mother possessed, to Margaret every thing was either black or white, she may not have felt threatened by this man but she still felt uneasy at not been able to understand the way he talked, felt or thought.

On reaching the crossroads the now even stranger, stranger, said I will just go and rob mister Blacklock's post office, that will get me the money for your mum, so see you in a short while. Margaret smiled and nodded her head as if In acceptance, then headed for the front door of the swan, her smile got weaker the further she walked and by the time she had reached her destination her face had moved on to a worried frown. Standing in the doorway his last words wouldn't go out of her head. Would he be stupid enough to break the law, just to get money for a night's lodgings, and if he did, how would he expect to get away with it? Could anyone possibly be so stupid, surely not? Then Margaret started to remember something that happened in nineteen sixty four when a young local lad came in and asked her mum to change two pounds of sixpences into pound notes. Her mum not seeing a problem did so taking the lads word for granted that he just wanting his savings changed to make it lighter for himself when he went to his grandmothers for his holidays. Only the next day she was visited by the police to be informed that the light clock meter for the snooker table in the reading room, only a matter of a few yards away had been robbed of all its sixpences and had she seen anyone acting suspicious. Needless to say they caught the lad right away. Watching him making a bee line for the post office she was just beginning to wish today had never started, when, a few moments later she new for sure.

Still Spellbound with her thoughts she watched him enter the post office, only to her horror a minute or so later she saw a hand place a sign in the window that read in big black letters big enough for her to see even at that distance CLOSED FOR DINNER.

Margaret opened the door and went over to her mum, who was about to say, seeing as how her daughter was empty handed. Could you not find him, but reading her daughters face again, changed it to, have you got a minute love in the kitchen. Away from the ears of her customers Peggy quietly said what's wrong now, could you not find him.

Not wanting to make any more of her seemingly daily ration of mistakes, explained to her mum every thing that had happened.

And you think that old man intends to rob the post office.

OH MUM, I don't now what to think anymore, but when has Mister Blacklock ever put up a closed sign in the window. I didn't even know he had one, he never closes for dinner, and he would open on Sundays if the post office would let him. Look Mum, all I am saying, is we moved in here ten years ago when I was twenty one, that was two years after he bought the post office, we have lived within a hundred yards of the post office all that time and mister Blacklock has never once had that sign in his window.

All right our Margaret I'll phone the police, though I don't know what they are going to say especially when I have just phoned them back to cancel that last fiasco with the band. Peggy picked up the phone and dialled 999 hello its me again, Peggy at the Swan, could I report that I think there's a chance Haybourgh sub post office is getting robbed, there was a pause, and then Peggy spoke again, yes, now as we speak, we think its an old man. There was another pause, and then Peggy carried on. What does he look like, oh you can't miss him he has long blond hair and a matching beard and wears a black duffle coat, and he looks just like a tramp.

Unawares of the entire goings on down the road, the stranger had opened the post office door to the sound of an alarm bell that rang every time someone entered the domain of mister Robert Blacklock. Bob to his friends. Bob was a slow quiet speaking ex police Sergeant who had done his twenty five years service with the force and in his wisdom had taken retirement at the young age of forty two. Also in his wisdom he took over the Hayborough sub post office on the retirement of the previous owner. Everything had worked out very conveniently and now at fifty four Bob was still in the prime of health, standing six foot four in his stocking feet and weighing in at a slim fourteen stone. He was still a hansom man with his thick dark hair and round happy rugged featured face. Tall dark and hansom, he was every woman's dream, just as he was every criminals nightmare. This dedicated man always put in one hundred and ten percent at what ever he did. Not recognising the rough looking stranger who was approaching his counter Bob looked a bit apprehensive, his old police instincts started to work overtime. What can I do you for, Bob asked the stranger?

Without a word the stranger handed Bob a small book. And as Bob opened it up a soft voice that didn't seem to go with the body said would you cash me a months payments please.

Bob recognised the slightly battered little red book having one almost identical himself. Reading the owners name on the inside page of the police pensions book, he raised his head and looked down into the eyes of the much smaller man who returned the unwanted stare without the blink of an eye.

The stranger said in his normal quiet voice, is there something wrong.

Bob Blacklock had never been known as a man of few words. The hardest thing about him, was stopping him talking and getting away from him. Not that you really wanted to, It was just that when he was a police man you knew which side of the fence he was on. Even off duty he was a policeman first, he was that good at his job you were never sure if you had been interrogated or not. In any passing conversation on the street you always felt you had given away some vital information, even when there wasn't any to tell. Bob Blacklock could talk for Britain, but for once he was speechless, his eyes left the smaller man and seemed to drift off into a dream, as they went back and studied the name on the inside cover, it was as if he was trying to build up some mental photograph to go along with the name. Raising his head, his eyes left the book and fell once more on his customer. Bob took in a deep lung full of air. The feelings he had inside felt as though he had been kicked in the stomach by a horse, breathing out the unwanted air he said in a well-shaken voice, it is you, isn't it. The stranger was about to become a stranger no more. Before the stranger could say I hope so or how do you know, Bob continued by saying, I never thought I would meet Kevin Hodgson in the flesh. The last time I heard of you, you were some were in America and that must have been three years ago, we all thought you must have died or something.

    Kevin asked, where did you here of me, and who were the, we all, you were talking about.

    Bob said the police gazette and every officer in the force, we all read about your exploits in America. With a shocked smile at the puzzled expression on Kevin's face Bob said are you trying to tell me you didn't know you were famous.

    Kevin replied it's the first I have heard about it.

    Bob shook his head saying they even had a nickname for you. You were called the Lone Ranger, the British one of course.

    Well, Kevin said, you learn a little every day, and I take it from the way you talk that you were also in the force.

    Twenty-Five of some good and some not so good years, mind you looking back even the bad years were good. Bob stopped himself from saying anything more his face being overtaken with remorse. Sorry. I really am sorry I wasn't thinking.

Don't take it to heart, what you said, was said in all innocence, it wasn't meant to hurt. What I have found in my case is that pain of the heart doesn't ease with time and there has got to be times when ghosts of the past catch up with me, I have found it very difficult if not impossible to hide from them, even if I fulfil my Promise I cannot foresee the ghosts ever going away. I am hoping to stay a day or two so maybe we can talk a little shop some time. I would like to hear what people have made up about me.

How about right now, Bob replied, delighted to make the offer, I don't normally close at dinner times but then theirs a first time for everything and to have two firsts in one day in this village can only be counted as a miracle. The only other thing that could happen today making it three in a row is for Jesus to walk threw that door and ask for an airmail stamped letter to Bethlehem. Both men got a giggle out of Bob's witticism.

Kevin liked what he saw in Bob and accepted his offer of the talk about old times.

Bob said, I better pay you your pension money, are you sure you just want one months because there's quite a lot to come.

No thanks, out on the road like we are the whole time Money doesn't mean a lot, we very rarely use it.

Bob said I suppose you don't have to pay rent or rates or anything that goes with a house. But that must be the only plus to living rough, I know I wouldn't do it. Opening a leather-covered book that looked important Bob spun it around to face Kevin and said, sign your Monica under the last entry for your money. As Kevin wrote his signature with his left hand, Bob unwittingly went to pass the money to Kevin's right hand. Realising and remembering Kevin's affliction to late, started to apologised profusely.

Don't be Embarrassed Kevin said, just hand it to the wife

she handles all my money. Your wife Bob said as he placed one hand on the counter to balance himself as he leaned forward to looked over Kevin's shoulder to see if she was standing out side the door. But Before Bob could do or see anything; the notes were pulled from his fingers and disappeared inside Kevin's duffle coat. Bob stepped back to see Kevin just finishing his signature, Looking puzzled Bob said, nice trick, in fact quite remarkable.

Looking up at Bob's expression, Kevin said no trick, as I said she handles all my money.

Bobs expression hadn't changed, as he said sorry I think I must have missed something somewhere.

Kevin said, most people miss what they don't expect to see, and normally I don't let people know anything more than what I think is necessary. As it is I think you are one of the people I would put on a need to know basis, so opening his coat, he pulled the right hand side back, saying Mister Bob Blacklock, please say hello to the wife.

Bob was astounded, for sitting in a specially made inside pocket was a wild female rabbit, her ears lay flat to her back and her nose twitched taking in the new smells that came from the human bean standing opposite. Well I never, did you ever see such a thing were all the words he could say. Then his wits coming together, Bob said, wont it chew the money into little bits.

Shaking his head Kevin said Bun never does anything bad she seems to know the difference between what is right and what is wrong. Which is more than can be said for some of the people I have met, closing his coat he said anyway that's enough talk about the wife how about that talk on old times.

Bob could see Kevin was very protected about his little rodent friend, but silently giggled to himself at the thought of how many pots of stew his wife had made out of the same ingredients. Fair enough he said, theirs an old sign inside that cupboard in the corner, take it out and stick it in the window, it will probably be a bit dusty by now because its never been out of there and in the window in all the time I have been here. Anyone seeing it will think I've some contagious disease or worse.

Kevin took the old sign that actually looked brand new and did what was asked of him then followed Bobs directions around the side of the counter and through a door into a large living room with a bay window, walking across the heavily carpeted floor Kevin headed for the window and stood there looking out over a sloping lawned garden with a perfusion of flowers around the four outer edges. A large rose covered rustic arch held a small latted gate in the bottom right hand corner which in turn led to a narrow path that came out somewhere between the cottages on Yukkies Brow. Kevin could see that someone didn't spend all his time in the post office, that's if it was Bob who did the gardening. From the comfy ness of the living room he could tell there was a strong female presence, perhaps he thought she was one of the ladies he saw on the bus, but then changed his mind. From the refineries he could see Bob and his wife were comfortably off and probably owned a car.

A whistle broke the silence with Bobs voice following, how do you like your tea, strong, weak or middling.

Middling came the reply, with two sugars and one milk.

A head popped threw the kitchen door, and asked the question, one milk, is that not a lot? Before the answer could be given Bob answered himself, its ok you can pore your own.

Bob brought in a large tray holding a full range of silver wear, from tea pot to milk, sugar, and even extra hot water, he placed the tray on an embroidered table cloth that half covered a one foot tall eighteenth century heavily polished table that conveniently served its purpose in front of the multi cushioned sofa. He then returned to the kitchen and produced a three-tier cake stand full of home made short bread and chocolate digestives.

Kevin thought this man is more refined than he looks, he maybe is the one that does the gardening, but for the love of me I cannot see him doing the cooking as well. He whispered into his coat, we are in a real classy house so don't make any crumbs when I hold you a short bread.

Mean while Back at the Swan, the lonely ladder that lent on the bedroom window sill were it had been left by its owner, was about to be joined by a white Morris minor van with pale blue doors and POLICE wrote on the side. Pulling up along side the ladder, two police officers in their late twenties got out. The driver went by the name of constable Jack Park, he stood an easy six foot on a leanly muscled body, his small round impish face was topped off with short straight mousy blond hair. The other officers resemblance stopped at his height, his name was constable John Shaw. His body had a larger frame than Jacks though not what you would call fat in any way, just more rounded and not built for speed. His hair was also straight but nearly black and slightly longer, his face had a kind softer more patient look the kind every mother wanted for a son in law. As they emerged from the van both constables donned on their helmets making them look even taller. Peggy and Margaret plus everyone else inside squeezed out the front door to meet them.

Constable Park being the more impatient was the first to speak. Right Peggy, we had a call from you saying a tramp was robbing the post office, is he still in there.

It's my fault Jack, Margaret piped in. I got mum to call.

Jack butted in. so this is just another false alarm like earlier this morning.

Peggy jumped to her daughters defence, saying, it most certainly is not Young Jack Park, and neither was it earlier on. If you had got here a bit quicker you might have found out. A little cheer came from the small crowd behind her and a voice whispered you tell them our Peggy.

Constable Shaw's calm voice broke in, so you managed to sort out this mornings problems on your own.

Well not exactly, I could have done, but the old man got their first.

The old man, constable Shaw repeated.

Yes the old man, you know the tramp that is robbing the post office.

Constable Park said, so their really is some one robbing the post office after all.

Margaret said, look Jack I'm not sure, he said he was going to rob the post office to get money to pay mum for a nights lodgings.

Streuth Peggy, Constable Shaw gasped out, how much do you charge these days to stay the night.

Ha, Ha, Peggy replied.

Jack looked at John and said I will take the back door if you take the front, and if you stay here Peggy and watch to see if either of us make the sign of a telephone like this, and he made a fist with his right hand, but leaving his thumb and little finger sticking out he stuck his thumb to his ear with his little finger touching his lips, if we do that, phone for help right away. OK, Peggy nodded, and the two constables took off. John Shaw moving faster than his size would have predicted, went to the right of the gas lamp and the shorter distance to the front door, was as Jack Park went to its left and down the hill to the rear gate.

Constable Shaw was thinking of his own father who also ran a post office in the little village of Appleby some two hundred miles away, with a sick feeling in his stomach that wasn't due to the running, he wondered how he would act if this had been his fathers post office, with him in it.

The bottom half of the post offices main and only window was frosted, so constable Shaw taking a little time to get his breath peeped over it at the corner of the building. Looking into the empty shop, the doors to both the living room and the kitchen were closed, and the only sign to recent life was the never before used, closed for dinner sign. Don't remember ever seeing that before John thought as he left the window and went to listen at the letterbox in the front door. Pushing the flap open with his fingers he put his ear to the opening, he could definitely hear voices coming from behind the living room door but could not make out what was being said, then something funny struck him, why would a post office have a letterbox in the front door surely the post man always took the letters to the counter when he picked up the mail. Taking off his helmet so he could get closer to the letterbox, John put it down on the pavement and then pushed his ear tighter to the letterbox he tried to hold the inside flap open as far as his fingers would allow, and tried to concentrate on the voices to see if he could pick up on any part of a conversation. It seemed impossible; the only things he could hear were muffled voices, nothing that sounded violent at all. Then without warning he heard a whisper in his ear.

What are you doing policeman Shaw.

The unexpectedness of the voice made Constable Shaw spring to his feet, the trouble was he only got half way as he found to his pain, trapping his fingers with the inside flap as the strong spring came into action with the sudden release of the pressure of his fingers. John gave out a stifled groan as the flap dug into his skin.

Quickly he pushed in his other hand to free his bleeding fingers, then took out a hankie and wrapped it around them to stem the flow of blood. Standing beside him was five-year-old Jimmy Findlay who lived opposite the post office, and had been off school through sickness. Spying his most favourite constable through the window had sneaked out to talk to him.

Jimmy, the officer said, you shouldn't be out here without your mum. And leading him by the hand, John walked the infant back to his mother's front door that stood slightly ajar. Opening the door wider, John walked in and called Babs.

A voice came back from the kitchen, is that you John, what's wrong. On seeing little jimmy she guessed what had happened and apologised.

Look Babs, I haven't got time to give him a talk because we are on official police business at the post office, so what ever you do please keep your doors locked until we find out what's going on, if anything, OK.

Babs said, ye sure, don't worry; he is confined to barracks as from this very second. As PC Shaw closed the door and ran across to the post office, he could here Babs say, Jimmy, get up to your room and just wait till your father gets home.

At the back door P C Park had ran all the way up the little high hedged track that lead to the back of the post office. He opened the little latted gate and had expected a squeak from its hinges, but not a sound came from the little gate. Instead a thorn from the rambling rose bush caught him across his right cheek drawing blood, and left a six-inch scratch. As the garden was on a slope there was really no need to hide from the rear windows but he stooped down anyway. On reaching the back door, he found despite his own height the windows still to high to see into without having something to stand on, so finding the back door unlocked he opened it slowly and peered inside. The kitchen was empty but he could hear voices coming from behind the living room door. Remembering a film he once saw, he picked up a glass from the sink and placed the open end carefully and quietly on the living room door, and putting his ear to the bottom of the glass, listened to what was being said. It only took a second to realise that the conversation was one of only normal chitchat, not robberies or violence. But taking nothing for granted Jack opened the door that led to the post office and P C Shaw. Climbing over the counter Jack crossed to the public side to open the front door. Looking through the glass door at John, he put his fingers to his lips intimating for him to be quiet, then mouthed that he believed every thing was ok but he wanted to catch out old ex sergeant Blacklock, Just for old time sake. Both policemen remembered Bob Blacklock from there early days as cadets, and even though he had always a reputation for being an extremely nice man, Jack thought to catch him out in his own home would get one over on him and be a laugh when retold back at the station.

Everything went wrong the second Jack opened the door, even before John could put one foot inside, the little alarm bell sounded and the impressive large frame of Bob Blacklock filled the now open living room doorway.

Before they could say anything, Bob, looking at their injuries, said, if you two young lads have had an accident, you're in the wrong place; this is a post office not the cottage hospital.

P C Shaw looked at his counter part and shook his head, then said, sorry Mr Blacklock we were investigating a report of a robbery-taking place and we.

Bob cut short, Shaw's explanation, saying a robbery, here, who's supposed to be robbing the place the invisible man.

Both PCs said nothing but looked past him at his guest sitting on his sofa.

Turning and looking at Kevin, Bob remembering his own first impressions.

Before he could say a word, Kevin stood up and walked towards him saying, I think I know what caused this mistake, I better go and make my excuses to her, and then I will show the wife a few of the local sights. Perhaps we can finish our little talk over a drink in the swan before I move on.

Nodding in forced agreement at the untimely ending of his most pleasurable dinner time for a long time Bob stepped into the post office in order to let Kevin through. For a split second Kevin looked tiny as he passed between the much larger three men. And to the sound of the once again activated bell P C Shaw opened the door and let Kevin out. Without a word Kevin stepped out into the fresh air and headed for Margaret and the small crowd of people who were now trying to get back into the swan.

When The bell stopped its cry, proving the door had returned to its closed position, Bob carried on watching him walk away for a few seconds, then turning to the two puzzled faces, gave his own feelings away by the more than sad look that clouded his normally happy face.

Chapter seven. The Strangers Story.

Jack broke the ice by saying, you know that old man.

Bobs answer was slow and subdued in coming. Not personally until today, but I do know all there is to know about him, at least probably more than most anyway. From little boy to old man he has become, stopping his words in mid sentence he said, you know he isn't as old as he looks.

Jack butted in, was he a villain from the old days.

No Jack you couldn't be further away from the truth, in fact the complete opposite. Look. You two better come and sit down because I think Kevin is one person the both of you should know about, that's if you can make the time and don't drip any blood on the carpet, I don't want any ear ache from our lass when she gets home.

John said we are investigating a robbery Bob and if you can give us any information on our main suspect then we can make all the time in the world to listen.

Bob asked, have either of you heard the name Kevin Hodgson before.

John was sure it rang a bell but Jack was the opposite.

Bob continued, well, what if I added Detective Sergeant to the front of his name, would that help.

It certainly would John said, so I take it that was him.

Jack had also grasped the importance of the Detective Sergeant and repeated what john had remarked, so that was him.

Yes that was him in the flesh, though theirs not as much flesh as I would have expected. I have followed Kevin's life story as though it were the bible and when you see him in real life, he must be about eighteen inches shorter than his reputation.

Before Bob could say more John asked the question, what's he doing around here?

Bob said you might know some things about Kevin, but probably not the things before you were born.

Before we were born Jack repeated.

Yes, exactly that, nearly thirty-two years to be exact. I was here at the time but I cannot remember ever meeting him. There were so many new faces drafted in because of the disappearance of the three little Clark sisters. The oldest was nine years old and the other two were five and six. It had been wrote up as abduction, then as the days went by it started looking more as if we were never going to find them and it was looking more like murder. Kevin was a seventeen-year-old cadet at the time and one of the hundreds of extras. There must have been two thousand civilian searchers, and at the time it was one of the biggest manhunts ever. For three weeks we searched day and night and found absolutely nothing then at the start of the forth week a seventeen year old cadet named Kevin Hodgson found them, all dead. It wouldn't have been a pretty sight and it wouldn't have been something a seventeen year old could have forgot in a hurry.

Jack asked, where did he find them, and then added quickly, had they been dead long.

They had been dead from the very first day, thinking out loud he said again only quieter yes the very first day. It was so sad, Kevin was searching about two miles from here along the banks of the dog gravy, you know the bit I mean that one hundred yard stretch of natural overflow for the river Ellen that has the railway to its back and the river to its front. No one thought it possible they could have been in there. According to a witness Kevin suddenly ran into the water, he seamed to know exactly where to go and within seconds had found the oldest, mind you he nearly lost his own life, there was so much mud it was like quick sand. When they got him out he was almost dead but still hanging on to the little girls body. They asked him at the inquest why he hadn't waited for help, he said I just thought there might be a chance she would still be alive, I couldn't wait. When the divers went in the same day and found the other two little girls, they had to have ropes tied to them and secured to the railway lines with helpers standing there ready to pull them in for there own safety. They said they didn't know how Kevin got out alive it was so sticky. A fortnight later after the autopsy, it was confirmed as accidental death and their bodies released for burial. The parents asked for Kevin to be at the funeral and the same day a service was held in the memorial gardens were Kevin Paid for the tree that was planted in the memory of the little girls. I don't know how someone seventeen years old could handle so much stress, mind you from that day on, he went up and up the ladder until he made detective sergeant were he stayed due to his own admission, he said once you go past detective sergeant you loose touch with reality. He had to be out on the streets, it kept him feeling alive. Then everything changed for the bad about ten years ago. Bob stopped for a second to come up for air, as he started remembering events that had taken place, he had imagines developing inside his head, they where ones he had never expected or wanted to see again. His face had started to pale as he looked at the quiet pair who had sat there without saying a word for some time. He felt like a school teacher giving a couple of kids extra tuition.

Deeply Engrossed in the whole saga Jack impatiently asked, what happened next.

What happened next, Bob repeated. You may well ask? Trying to put the pictures that were forming to the back of his mind Bob continued where he had left off. Yes, it was ten years ago, Kevin's son had decided to move to Scotland with his wife and eight month old daughter, and the problem started when a loan shark he had borrowed money off to purchase a car got it into his head that he was going to do a runner and he wasn't going to get the seventy pounds that was still outstanding. So in his wisdom he either sold the dept too, or paid three heavies to collect the car or the money before they could move. His choice wasn't very good, the men he picked were all fresh out of jail and complete nutters, anyway the following morning Kevin's daughter in law called at the loan sharks office and paid the money in full which should have ended it before it got started.

The problem was the loan shark couldn't get a hold of the hit men and they carried on with their job. A few hours later they caught up with Kevin's son and when he didn't have the money on him they said they where taking the car, he explained the money had been paid, but of coarse not believing him, tried to take the car. He put up a brave fight against impossible odds, before ending up beaten unconscious and thrown in the boot of his own car. As they drove away Kevin's granddaughter who was on the back seat in her cot started to cry, and then to cap it all one of the three remembered whose son he was and as they where all out on parole, which meant that for the least criminal offence they would be returned to prison to serve the rest of their terms without even getting a trial. They all agreed they couldn't allow that to happen, they wouldn't take the chance he might talk, it ended up that Kevin's son and granddaughter were never seen again.

Were their no witnesses John asked?

Oh yes, plenty, the whole thing took place on the main street of a village much the same as Hayborough, but you know what its like, the heavies were all well known local men and no one wants to get involved in case they end up being next.

John pushed back in again asking, how do you know so much then if there weren't any witnesses.

Bob looked at John and said that's right there weren't any official witnesses that would come forward and testify but there was one unofficial witness. When Kevin was a kid, times were hard, it was so much harder to survive then than now. He mixed with all the wrong kids because he was one of the wrong kids and if you were a friend of his he stuck by you no matter what. Every friend he had, stayed a friend, when he jumped the gap to be a police cadet. Mind you give the man his due he told them face to face that their business would become his, if they operated on his territory. And sure enough his friendship must have meant a lot because his area was virtually crime free all the time he was there. Which was more than could be said for the rest of us.

It was Jacks turn to put in his two penny worth, saying probably you got all his problems.

Were upon Bob replied, true enough we did catch a few villains from his side of the county line, but that was only a tiny amount of what we suspected. Anyway to clear up Johns question, one boy hood friend who wasn't what you could call a real villain, at least lets say he was to clever to catch, said he would help. Now this feller was built like a brick outside loo, and he was so good with his fists, to say he was a hard case, having no sense of fear was an under statement, but as I told you this friend also had brains. Within a week, he had all the information I just told you, but he told Kevin it had to be off the record. He said it wouldn't have bothered him to go in the ring with Rocky Marciano, but these three men didn't stay on the same planet as them selves, they took cattle drugs to build up their muscles, and even though he believed natural strength and fitness was far better than manufactured, he said he wasn't sure if even he could handle the three of them. Because of the drugs, their minds were distorted so much they had lost all knowledge of reality and what was right and wrong, and as he had a family to think of he had to be on the safe side and keep his information off the record. He told Kevin about the seventy pound dept, and how his son was beaten up and thrown in the boot, and he believed, that Kevin's son was taken to a lonely part of the west Cumberland coast line were he was made to dig a hole big enough for himself before being beaten again for good measure and the fun of it, then tied up and thrown in and buried. Kevin was told that this last bit was an educated guess because he had been told of a young man who had gone through the same treatment, but had managed to escape at the last minuet because the same three men were so high on some other kind of drug. He had relived his story to a friend before moving down to London and changing his name.

The baby girl, what happened to her?

The baby girl, Bob repeated. Bob was so deep in his own story that the questions coming back to him sounded distant and dreamlike, he heard them but they didn't register in his brain until he woke himself up by repeating the question and taking a second or two to think about it. Sorry John I was miles away, what was it you asked, oh yes the baby girl, that was it. Well she was never seen again, the best that could have been hoped for was that she was given away secretly to someone desperate for a baby, probably someone who for some medical reason couldn't have one of there own. The trouble with that theory is, there would be to many loopholes and the three heavies no matter how fuddled their brains were wouldn't want to leave anything to chance. If a grave is ever found, you can bet your cotton socks the baby would be lying next to her dad. The car was never found, the best men in the force searched from lands end to John o groats but not a trace any were. They searched every scrap yard. Giving the ones with a crusher a double going over, they came up with zilch. If the force ever felt inadequate it was then, maybe some day someone will stumble on something by accident and solve the case but that's no more than wishful thinking on my part.

Jacks cheeky round boyish face had changed, as he sat there on the sofa a hard blank expression had taken its place, you could see he had justice and murder on his mind. His open mouth when it did find the motivation to speak, spoke angrily but with sympathy, it's a wonder that old man can sleep at night with everything he has on his mind, who can blame him for wondering the roads like a tramp, he probably doesn't know which way to turn and just keeps following his nose.

Oh, Jack, if it had only stopped there it would have been so much of a blessing. But it didn't, it just grew worse, in fact worse than worse it became a living nightmare and Kevin blamed himself for bringing it down on his family. Well I ask either of you, what would you have done under the same circumstances.

Kevin believed he knew everything but could prove nothing; it was driving him to the edge. He started hounding the three heavies day and night; he would have done them for their dog fouling the pavement if it meant getting them put away.

Remember if they broke the law once, they would be sent back to serve the rest of their original sentence and once inside we could have made it harder for them to get out, in fact, really hard.

    One night about three months later, three men wearing balaclavas broke into Kevin's house while he and his wife Janet were asleep. Two of them had sawn off shotguns and the third carried a machete. For big men they moved quietly, because the first thing Kevin and Janet knew was being woken up by the bedroom light coming on and finding sawn off shotgun barrels pressed firmly under their chins. He knew who they were by the size of them, but without clear identification because of the balaclavas it would never have held water in court. Anyway two of them dragged Kevin out of bed and tied him in the sitting position to his bed side chair. They gagging him for good measure with one of his own socks stuffed in his mouth and held it there with the help of his own trouser belt. Once they had Kevin immobile, they turned their attentions to Janet, who in her stocking feet wouldn't have stood five foot. They tied her wrists and ankles to the four corners of the bed with dressing gown belts and what ever else of that ilk they could find in the wardrobe. They told Kevin they weren't going to gag her because they wanted him to hear every groan and moan that was about to come out of her tiny mouth. Every time Kevin tried to get out of the chair, one of them would hit him square in the face with the butt of his shotgun nearly knocking him unconscious. Kevin remembered one of the gang saying, not too hard man, we want him to be able to see or at least hear what we do to her. Laughing they started tearing Janet's night clothes off, and once she was naked took it in turns to rape her over and over again.

    Kevin said at Janet' inquest,

    John stopped Bob in his tracks saying, God man they killed her.

    Bob answered, yes they did, but not right away, though it would have been more merciful if they had have done, but to be honest these guys didn't know the meaning of the word.

John could see he had broken Bobs stride, and said Sorry Bob carry on.

Bob looked a little lost for a second then said, were was I, oh yes, at the inquest Kevin said Janet hadn't really made much noise of any kind and they seemed to get disappointed and bored with what they were doing, then one of them said lets see if we can make her jump with this and picked up the machete from the floor. Holding the blade he placed the handle between her open legs and said three two one here I come and forced the handle as far as he could Inside her.

Kevin said it was pity full the cries that cam out of her but just like mercy they also knew no pity. He said he tried to get out of the chair and was expecting another bang in the face with the shotgun but they took no notice of him because they each wanted to take a turn at their newfound game.

Then one of them thought up a new use for the machete and said out loud looking at Kevin lets shave her.

Stuff that, came back a reply, where's the fun in that, lets scalp the bitch. Where abouts he grabbed the machete from his partner in crime and said you two hold her legs because this is going to make her really jump. And that's what they did, two big brave men held her still while the other scalped her of her pubic hair. The pain or the lack of blood or both must have been to much for her, because half way through this knew terror Janet passed into unconsciousness which was just as well because as the one who had scalped her rubbed the bloody pubic hair scalp in Kevin's face the other two decided there wasn't much left they could do to degrade Janet except one thing. So leaning from both sides they proceeded to each cup one of her tiny breasts in their large hands and seeing as how she was unconscious and could feel no pain took a bet as to who would be the fastest to bite off a nipple. Lifting up their balaclavas to nose height. They bit, chewed and tugged till one came out the winner, and when both had succeeded they went across to Kevin showing the nipples between their front teeth and said remember these sunshine, take a good look, because it's the last time you'll ever see them. Then as if previously rehearsed, laughing together they swallowed them.

Right lets do what we came here to do, said the one who must have been their leader. And without warning he hit Kevin a vicious blow to the temple with his gun butt knocking him semi conscious, and unable to do anything to defend himself. Then they released his right arm and rested it on the bedside table. Kevin remembered someone saying this is one way to shorten the long arm of the law and brought down the machete chopping through his hand at the base of the thumb, when the blade was lifted there were still some skin tissue holding the two part together so the man with the blade said I like to do a tidy job when I do one and ran the blade over the joining tissues severing the two parts for ever. I think that was a good nights work said a voice that drifted into Kevin's head, and then the last thing he remembered before he passed out was a voice laughing, saying, try feeling my collar now copper.

It wasn't until the next day when Kevin didn't arrive for work and couldn't be contacted by phone that alarm bells started to ring. They didn't ring very loud at first but loud enough for a constable to be sent on a pushbike.

A pushbike Jack gasped out.

Yes, I know what you are going to say, but in those days we didn't have the resources we have today and to be honest I still don't think we would have them today if it wasn't for what happened that night in nineteen fifty nine.

Kevin's house was quite a long way out in the country side and it took the local bobby on the beat about half an hour to just peddle there, and remember the local beat bobbies were always young new raw recruits, and got moved around from one beat to another regularly so as to help them not make to many good friends that might compromise them in the job they were doing. They were to be honest inexperienced, and the lad they sent out was no different. When the young constable finally got there he found signs of the front door being forced and not wanting to disturb any clues cycled two miles back to the nearest phone box to report what he had found and what did they want him to do next. Which as it happened was the best thing he could have done because if it had been a normal break in it would have been up to him to deal with it himself, but because of it being Kevin's house the office told him to get back and hold the fort and not disturb anything until C I D got there. When they did get there they didn't expect to find what they did, in fact I don't think any one could have been ready for what they found. Janet had obviously bled to death because of her horrific injuries and was just covered up until the photographer arrived to take photos for evidence. Kevin how ever had been lucky, mind you not that he looked at it that way at the time. Anyway some how his blood had clotted around his damaged hand and even though he was nearly dead due to loss of blood he ended up making as full a recovery as was possible under the circumstances.

  John and Jack both wanted to speak together but John got in first, were we able to make an arrest on the strength of what Kevin could tell us.

  Bob shook his head and took a deep breath, I think even if Kevin had seen their faces we would still not have had a case. First of all we were up against organised crime, well planed, and

  Well, finished off.

  Jack impatiently butted in, but it was obvious who they where by the descriptions, surely it was just a matter of bringing them in and wearing them down, they would have talked sometime.

  First of all Jack, Kevin didn't see their faces so without good evidence their solicitor or I should say in their case Barrister, would have claimed victimisation and he would have had a point because it was well known that Kevin had hounded the three of them, and their Barrister would simply say he was lying threw his teeth just to get them, especially since they were all on holiday in Spain at the time of the crime.

Both P C s said together. They were on holiday in Spain, so they didn't do it after all.

Bob came back at them again, its what I said before, O C, Organised Crime, they did it all right, its just we couldn't prove how they did it. They had some way planed to get back here from Spain to do the crime and the same for a return journey. In the first place it took us three days to find out they were in Spain, which gave them all the time in the world to get back, and when we pulled them at the air port all the people who were with them said they were all together at some over night party on the night in question. Apart from that there wasn't one clue at the scene of the crime, everything they brought with them they took with them, everything they used to tie Kevin and Janet up with belonged to Kevin and Janet. There wasn't even any bloody footprints, as all the blood from Janet was soaked into the bed and Kevin's had only just started to flow when they left. No lads, we could not even get a foothold, no matter how hard we tried. I think Sherlock Holmes would have been stumped on this one. Just as Kevin did before, we knew everything, but could prove nothing. Kevin got pensioned off supposedly because of his disability. He could have done a desk job not to mention getting a false hand, and going for inspector. I think the top and bottom of it, was the big brass thought that after all he had gone through he may not have been stable, and just might cause the force some embarrassment. As it was, Kevin didn't have to be pushed, he seemed more than willing to leave, with all his troubles no one would have blamed him if he had have gone over the top and fallen to pieces, but he didn't, he made a complete u turn. With all the spare time he had, he concentrated on learning any and all forms of self defence, any kind of unarmed combat at all in fact he said in his case it was one armed combat. He ended up with one main one, Karate, he said it suited him the best though it wasn't really what he wanted because it didn't allow him to use every part of his body to win, he said never again would he let any man get the upper hand on him.

Chapter Eight.
The Promise.

Kevin said Karate would have to do for now, but he was still looking for that something better, that upper hand, a self defence of which there was no defence. By now every one that knew him knew why he was pushing himself so hard, he had made Janet a promise the day he laid her to rest. It took only four people to carry her tiny coffin, but it took six to carry Kevin. A friend of mine who was there said it was so pity full to see, he was so distraught he cried like a child for three days, right up until he watched her lowered into her final resting place. He wouldn't leave until the last shovel full of soil had filled her grave; he said he had to watch to make sure she was safe from the hands of man. As the last shovel full was spread over her grave, the people who stayed with him, which also including the grave diggers saw him raise his good arm in the air and making a fist, Kevin looked up to the heavens and shouted. If you can find the time to listen, I have a challenge for you. My little lady never hurt a fly, yet you let her be defiled and her defilers go free. I shall give her justice and your defilers will suffer that justice, stop me if you can. He left no doubt in any ones mind as to what he meant, though they were never sure whom he was addressing. God or the devil, I don't think he cared; he just blamed anyone and everyone that stood up in front of him, as anyone who fought him found out. Kevin's policy seemed to be, the best defence Is Attack. His Karate went from strength to strength, he entered every competition there was going and he won every bought.

He started getting famous and had a large following and he got so good he was asked to fight for Britain in the world Karate championships in Japan. Well even on a police pension Kevin just couldn't afford to go, he was spending his money as fast as he got it anyway going to all the local and national events.

When the local papers got hold of the story they started to ask for sponsors and before Kevin knew what hit him the whole town, had, had a collection and raised enough money to send him to Japan three times over. The faith they had in him was proved right; he went through his opponents as if they were water. Right up until the semi final were he got disqualified for what the judges called over reacting. I got told, by someone who was there, that he had been lucky, not to have been thrown out long before then. The judges as every one else were of the opinion that Kevin wasn't just trying to score points from his opponents he was trying to destroy them. The drawing of blood was not allowed on purpose, the places for scoring points were bloodless but Kevin always managed to draw blood and when he saw it the judges said he seemed to go out of control. The one man Kevin wanted to fight was a little Chinese American called Lee. He had watched him from the start, but never got picked to go against him, in fact it was he that came out the winner and took the title back to America. Kevin said he couldn't believe how fast he was and for a tiny man his punching power was devastating, he seemed to be supercharged and for once he had found someone who may even have not only had more willpower than himself but more everything than himself. Kevin didn't know exactly what he himself was looking for from karate, but whatever it was Mister Lee seemed to have it.

    Kevin was disappointed to say the least, as he headed for the airport and home, he was sure he had let the people back home and himself down by not winning. He was calling himself every useless thing under the sun when destiny threw him a lifeline. As Kevin entered the airport an oriental man stood at the reception desk holding above his head a large square piece of card painted with tall letters that spelled the name Kevin Hodgson. Kevin introduced himself to the oriental and he in turn said that his master had been watching him at the competitions and wanted him to return to his school for training. Kevin took it all as a joke and laughing politely said I'm sorry, not today, and took out his return flight tickets and handed them to the lady receptionist were upon the little oriental said.

    So sorry, Master Lee will be disappointed.

Kevin turned to the oriental, his eyes and ears now wide open said Master Lee, is that the same Master Lee that just won the world Karate championships.

The oriental said nothing just nodded.

Kevin said but I am on my way home to England.

Were upon the oriental said in broken English, it is your choice sir and bowed his head as if to walk away.

Kevin said, wait I need more time to think.

The oriental smiled and said, sometimes the mind has questions of the future were as the heart can only give you answer off the past, it is up to you Master Kevin as to whether you follow your mind or your heart, which ever you follow your plane leaves in a small time.

You mean if I don't go back to England I wont be staying here.

Yes Master Kevin, my Masters home is in America and the ticket for your flight is here, you only have to say yes.

Kevin looked at the receptionist and said, sorry, I wont be needing, that return ticket after all, it looks like I'm going to America.

And that was how it happened, he took the ticket and headed to where his mind was hoping to get answers and his heart was hoping to get piece, and that was about the last time we heard from him. The odd story came out in the police gazette telling us how he was training the police over there in the art of self defence and how they had given him the nick name of the English Lone Ranger. The next we Knew, he had moved with that Master Lee to Hong Kong and that was the last we heard of him from that day to this.

P C Shaw looked at P C Park and said I don't know about you but I feel sick to my stomach. If I didn't know it was true, I would have said the whole story was unbelievable. And sometimes we think we have problems, what that man has gone through is no ones business. Anyway what happened to the bad guys, did they ever get brought to justice?

Shaking his head Bob said with malice in his voice they are still out there and that's the problem, some day Kevin will meet up with them and every one knows what is going to happen. There is no way Kevin is going to break the promise he made to Janet; myself I hope it never happens.

Jack looked Bob up and down and shaking his head disbelieving and a little angry said you don't want justice.

Bob replied sharply, of coarse I do, but through proper channels. Where's the justice if Kevin ends up getting life, because that's what you get for pre meditated murder.

Jack pushed the fingers of his left hand though his short blond hair, and looking sheepish, said sorry Bob I wasn't thinking, I can see what you mean, but they just cannot get off Scot-free. Hell, I feel as though I could kill them myself.

Bob stopped Jack from saying anything else by trying to give him some good advice. Listen son, in this game never take it to heart, you win some, and you loose some. Kevin took it to heart because I suppose he thought he had no choice, and under the same circumstances I don't know that anyone else and that includes me, would have done anything different. But with hind sight, and that's the only way we can look at it now, if he had backed off, then Janet would still be alive today.

The only trouble with that theory John exclaimed, was that it was the, what come first, the chicken or the egg. Kevin was in a catch twenty-two situation. Oh it doesn't bare thinking about. Look Bob, we better go, we have a lot of explaining to do when we get back.

Ye and I better open up the shop it's a wonder my customers are not banging on the front door, they probably would have been, but by now the whole village will be waiting to find out the outcome of the great Hayborough post office robbery.

Jack feeling a bit more jovial said its ok we will tell Peggy and then everyone in the county will know the outcome in five minuets.

The two P C s got up and headed for the front door and

were greeted by the alarm as they opened it.

John Shaw said, just a minuet, I thought you were superstitious about not going out the door you came in.

Listen John Shaw, if you think I'm risking my life again trying to get passed those trained killer roses of his, you are sadly mistaken, though by the look of your hand maybe I should go out the way I came in. Hey Bob, did I hear Kevin say something about showing his wife the local sights, he must have got married again, I wonder what she looks like because I didn't notice her anywhere.

Bob gave a knowledgeable grin, she's not what you would expect Jack, and you wouldn't see her anyway, he keeps her in his inside pocket.

What do you mean, he keeps her in his inside pocket, is it a photo of Janet.

No Jack, what he calls his wife is a wild female rabbit that's been with him from a baby; she can't walk proper because of being attacked by a weasel. She does tricks and things, well anything he tells her to, and I shouldn't call them tricks because she seems to understand Kevin, and vice versa. She couldn't survive without his help and to be honest I don't think he could survive without hers, that's why I think he calls her the wife.

That's amazing John said, just amazing, and exhaling a big sigh, said, you know Bob, Hayborough might be a quiet back water, but for once, someone really has come to town.

Chapter Nine. Black Ada's Cottage.

Every one in the Swan was still watching As Kevin walked away from the post office, and seeing everything was all right, an embarrassed Margaret ran over to him apologising profusely. I'm so sorry, I didn't know whether you meant it when you said you were going to rob the post office; I had to tell the police.

Slow down doll, it's not your fault, if there is any blame its mine. I have a strange sense of humour, and unless you are on the same wavelength, my jokes can go clean over the top. I was brought up on the Marx brothers and later on the Goons with Spike Milligan. Their humour is just me, sometimes I talk the biggest, most utter load of rubbish, and if it gets a laugh, it gets one, if it doesn't, it doesn't, what odds. I sometimes say things, I don't know I am going to, I even baffle myself. A lot of years ago a lady came to visit us and I apparently said to her as she entered the house, for no reason at all, be care full of that plant on the side board because it bites. Now I had forgotten I had ever said it, but six months later she came on a return visit and I wasn't there. Janet had a hell of a time trying to convince her that there was no such plant and never had been before she would come in. So you see you have absolutely nothing to be sorry for.

That's ok for you to say but I have to make it up to you. I insist, so think of something you would like and if I can, I will.

Kevin thought for a second, then said ok, take me to the most romantic place you know.

It was one request she hadn't expected, and she found herself feeling a little worried. But she had offered and not wanting to go back on her word, agreed. But for her safety, said, I better see if mum needs me for anything. and if she doesn't, we can go right away. As they headed back to the Swan, everyone who had been on the outside watching had disappeared, and on entering the front door they were all found to be in their former places. Margaret beckoned her mum to come to her end of the bar and out of the twitching ears of the locals. She felt like a small child asking for money for sweets. She asked if she could have an hour off to take the old man as far as the two hills, and in the same breath whispered to her mum why she was doing it. Not that she needed to, because as Zorro would have said, if Peggy hadn't been to close. Bat ears could hear through a locked door.

Peggy's answer was what Margaret expected. Of coarse you can love, we wont be busy until tonight anyway. Try and be back for teatime, you know how much your dad worries.

It took them only a few minuets to walk the length of the village and at the end of the street the little tarmac road bore left up a steep hill and pointing in that same direction was a white cast iron sign wearing the black painted letters and numbers that spelled Little Moor 3 miles, Great Moor 5 miles. Following the signs direction, the odd couple walked to the top of the hill were the road levelled out and turned right. The road passed a tiny toll cottage that stood on its right, and then carried on a little before turning left up an even steeper hill that seemed a stairway to the clouds.

Kevin, looking at the climb ahead, said I thought your mum wanted you back for tea.

Margaret, seeing the direction his eyes were looking said, no silly, we aren't going up there, we are going in here, and tugged at his coat sleeve pulling him in the direction of the toll cottages massive gate pillars. The cottage was in a state of disrepair, and showed all the signs of not been loved or lived in for a great many years. All the windows had lost the glass that protected the inside from the outside elements. The one and only door that had once faced out into what had been a low dry stone walled garden was missing all together. Peeping through the glassless void into the darkness, they could see were children had been rearranging rubble into some kind of order that resembled seats, an empty orange box sat in the middle, as if used as a table. In the far bottom left corner of this now wild and uncultivated garden, grew a row of six elderberry trees, whose branches were alive with thrushes and blackbirds taking advantage of their autumn harvest of a million tiny black berries whose weight seemed to be bending their producer to breaking point.

What happened to the lady that lived here, did she move? Margaret was taken aback, and replied with her own double question. You knew a lady lived here, how did you know.

Kevin smiled. My questions first, age before beauty.

Margaret blushed at the compliment, then said. Mum told me she died before I was born.

Before you were born, strewth, aw I'm, well that's taken the wind out of my sails. Ada couldn't have been much older than you are now when she died.

Margaret looked puzzled, how did you know she was called black Ada.

Black Ada, Kevin exclaimed, that's a new one on me. I only knew her as Ada, I didn't even know what her full name was, and I don't mean the black bit, I mean her sir name;. Look it doesn't really matter but it s just a shock to know she died not long after I knew her, that's all.

Margaret turned her back to the dry stonewall and sat on it. Realising they were staying put for the time being, Kevin did the same just as a flock of pigeons flew low, skimming the tops of their heads. Margaret ducked her head but Kevin never moved.

In front of them the grassy field rose to a small hill with a pigeon loft situated on the top. Its multi coloured woodwork stood out a mile, Kevin thought I must be getting old not to have noticed it until now.

Margaret said, stupid birds scared me half to death, I'm sure Murdock lets them out on purpose just to scare people walking by. Come on you haven't answered me yet, out with it.

Margaret had a lovely honest face that could charm anyone, but Kevin didn't need charming, he also was honest, and said there's not a lot to tell, well not about Ada anyway. It all started about thirty odd years ago, it seams like yesterday but it also seems like a dream. I was a police cadet, and I was drafted in with hundreds of other officers to help search for three missing little sisters, the oldest was only nine and the younger two were five and six. They looked lovely in the photos we saw; they had jet-black wavy hair right down their backs. We had been searching for them for nearly four weeks without any success, and one stormy night when we had abandoned the search I took shelter behind the side of this house while every one else ran for Hayborough. I had only been there a second when Ada came out for some logs that were stacked up against the wall that was sheltering me from the rain. In the darkness I scared her half to death, but once I explained who I was, and as I was in uniform anyway she asked me if I wanted to come inside until the rain eased off. So I helped her carry some fire wood in and she made me a hot very potent, what she called double elder flower wine, that probably came from those very trees there. I was soaked through to the skin so she told me to undress in her bedroom and gave me a robe to put on while my clothes were drying in front of the fire. I sat there in her robe and should have been dead with embarrassment if not for the wine that by now had zonked my brain into dreaming I was in heaven, I didn't wake up until five the next morning. I remember there were only red painted sandstone flags on the floor and the ashes from the fire covered the first row. At the time I thought see was older than my mother but looking back she was probably no older than you are now.

 OH thanks, you cheeky thing, Margaret said as see gave him a friendly push on his shoulder.

 No Margaret, I don't mean it like that, its just at the time, I was only seventeen, and when you are that age, some one twenty was classed as the older women never mind a lady in her thirties. I can see were she got the name black Ada from, because, from what I remember she didn't have very much except kindness, politeness and manners.

 It's nice to hear you say that, and I forgive you for calling me old, Ada was a close relative of ours, only mum always got a bit touchy when I tried to bring up the subject. Ada was not only known as black Ada, but also the black sheep of the family. Margaret went silent for a second, then changed the direction of their conversation, saying. They found the girls dead, didn't they?

Ye, only a few days later, and with the case looking accidental we were all moved back to our divisions. I came up here to say goodbye and thanked Ada for her kindness. She started to cry and said no one had ever been as nice to her as I had, she then went and pulled out a small tin that was behind a loose stone in the back of the fireside cupboard. She put her hand in the tin and then forced something into my pocket as a keepsake. It must have been the only thing of value she had. I wrote to her a few times but never got any reply; I thought she must have moved away or something.

Margaret said it was probably the something.

The something, I don't get you Margaret, what did I miss.

The one thing I did find out about Ada, was she could hardly read or write so if she had got any letters from you she wouldn't have known what to do with them.

Their conversation was broken by the starting up of a constant whistling coming from Murdock's loft, it was his way of telling his feathered friends that it was time to come home and it was the break they needed to move on from black Ada's cottage.

They had only walked a few steps when Kevin asked, you know the guy who sold your mother the fish, I think his nickname was Scatter. Margaret nodded in recognition. Well he played a big part in finding those girls.

He did, Margaret said sounding surprised, he never said.

Kevin smiled and said he probably never knew. I used to watch him all those years ago doing what he called snigging fish. Anyone else would call it poaching, but snigging made it sound more like a profession and more legal. I asked him how he managed to snig a trout nearly every time he cast into the river, and he told me he could see them, and once he started pointing out a few things I seemed to pick it up real quick. Everything he said made sense, different colours, shadows, things that should and shouldn't be there, he said he didn't mind telling me because I was no threat to his lively hood. Well a few days later I had the chance to put everything he had told me into practice. I was walking along the banks of what you all call the Dog Gravy and I noticed something dark in the water and just below were I was standing, I spotted a broken branch and some sods disturbed below the branch. The bank was really steep there and I just knew the shadow was one of those girls. It looked as though the oldest had fallen in first and the two little ones had tried to get her out and couldn't get back up the bank. They must have been all of three miles from their home and no one saw them at any time, even after all this time I still find it so hard to believe that not one single person had noticed them. Never mind the fact that what were they doing there anyway, what made them walk all that way to somewhere they had never been. One moment they are in their back garden the next drowning in the dog gravy, it just doesn't make sense. They had to cross roads, walk along a main street, climb over farm gates, it was as if something just plucked them out of their garden and dropped them in the water.

Margaret could see the old man was getting more and more upset, and tried to change the subject, perhaps it was just the police man in you, you know what they say, once a police man, always a police man.

Ye, you are probably right, its just that when I get a new ear that listens I end up bending it to far.

Margaret could now see the sadness in his face, but she also felt it coming from the depth of his sole. Her Mum had been so right when she had read his face in the Swan. In the innocence of youth, she took it, that it was, he had questions that he could never have answers to, and they were still weighing heavy if not getting heavier on his mind. She had to change the subject all together.

Chapter Ten. The White Lady
And The H Tree.

Look at those trees, aren't they lovely; dad says he collected conkers off them when he was a kid. They must be a hundred years old, maybe more.

Looking down the winding track at the distant horse chestnuts, he said, they were probably planted when the hall was built and that had got to be at least a minimum of four hundred years. The hall stood to the left of the track, its majestic castle like appearance ran the length of a football pitch, and could have come right out of a movie.

Margaret shook her head as in disbelief. Four hundred years, that's a long time, just think of all the stories they could tell. The one opposite the hall gates is a ghost tree, they call it the H tree because its got a H sign in the bark and if you walk around it one hundred times at midnight on Christmas eve the white lady appears in that window above the hall main gates.

Have you ever seen her, came back the question.

No I was always in bed waiting for morning and the presents by the fire hearth, mind you there have been stories of people who have. Mum told me the story came about when at one Christmas Eve party the Dixon family played a game of hide and seek. One women went into an unused store room and got into an air tight travel trunk and when she pulled the lid down she found out it was self locking. With all the drink and merry ness going on, no one realised she was missing until it was far too late.

Kevin Said with quite a lot of laughter in his voice, I've heard stories like that before.

Come on if you don't believe me, come and look for your self and she started to run the one hundred and fifty yards. Giggling like a child. Margaret looked really fit as her long legs sprinted flat out across the grassy field.

Taking up the challenge, Kevin held his bad hand tight across Bun to stop her from being shaken about. Within fifty yards Kevin was running level and both were in fits of hysterical laughter, the only difference between them was she was starting to weaken fast, where as he was getting stronger. By the time she had gone eighty yards, she found herself out of breath and coming to a standstill, she didn't even have the strength to laugh. Looking ahead, Margaret could see the old man was still laughing and nearly at the tree.

Turning to look at Margaret, he found himself alone, smiling he said, it looks like we've still got it were it counts, though I don't supposed you cared much for all that juggling about.

Reaching the tree and still out of breath Margaret gasped, were you in the Olympics or something, I never saw anyone run like that never mind some one. She stopped for a second, as she was about to say, as old as you, but changed her mind, not wanting to offend and simply said wearing a duffel coat.

He knew what she was going to say and it wouldn't have offended him if she had said it, because just like Bob Blacklock's remark, it was said in all innocence, but what made it nicer, was the point that she thought it would hurt his feelings and stopped herself in time from saying it and causing any embarrassment.

Twelve conker trees, they must have planted one for each month of the year, so where's this famous H tree then.

Right behind you and you haven't answered my question.

What question was that?

How come you can run so fast?

Kevin was still feeling silly and said I get a little help from some one who would normally do running for a living.

Margaret was quick with an answer for him, saying, who's that then BRAR RABBIT.

Close, Kevin said, Close.

See the H she said, and sure enough there was a nine inch square letter H on the west side of the tree, it wasn't carved there or put there artificially, it was simply made out of tree bark and was just some sort of unknown abnormality in the tree.

Well you were right, there it is as large as life, I suppose you are going to tell me that it stands for the white ladies name, Helen or something.

Margaret thought for a second, then said I don't know, I never thought about it like that, we can ask mum when we get back, she knows everything about everything and then some.

Feeling the bark with his good hand, as though caressing a beautiful lady, Kevin Looked up into the enormity of the giant tree whose branches just like the elder held a mother load of fruit. Isn't nature wonderful, I used to wonder were a tree keeps It's brain.

Replying to his back, Margaret said, trees don't have brains do they.

He turned around and faced her saying, that was the way I figured it, in the overall picture of things these fine ladies are like the lungs of the earth, giving out oxygen that keeps other things alive, I believe just like our brain tells our lungs to breath then the Earth tells its lungs to do the same. Think of all the other by products that this one-lady gives away free, and before you say firewood, that's not what I'm talking about. I mean things like the fruit she is bearing now that's starts new life and feeds small animals, the homes and nesting places for birds animals and insects, and at winter time she casts her leaves and puts back into the earth what she has taken out of it. Nature, Margaret, is a wonderful thing. The trouble is, nature never accounted for man in its scheme of things, and I believe man will be the beginning of the end for nature.

Margaret could once again see the pain in his eyes and hear the same in his voice, in the short time she had known him, she had found him different from any other man she had ever met. She wanted to say something but let him carry on, he seemed to be desperate to put his thoughts into words that she could understand well enough to then make her own.

Everything in nature asks for nothing except the food to live, and just like this lady behind me, helps in some way to help something else to live, were as man only wants to take away, he never gives anything in return except pollution.

    Margaret looked at his sad face, but had to say something. Surely we have a right to live as well, I mean we have been here just as long as everything else just like the bible says.

    I think the bible was probably given to man, by man, to help justify what ever he wants justified and as for being here as long as everything else, well I doubt it. If some one made man take off his clothes and live off the land, ninety five percent of the worlds population would be dead in less than the seven days the bible says it took to make the world. I don't think man ever evolved on this planet at all, if he had, he would know the meaning of Mother Nature.

    Margaret could see not only his point, but also how deep he was, the old man was a thinker, there was no point in trying to argue with him, his mind was made up and it looked as though it had been for many years. It did however hit her how much he hated his fellow man, if she had been able to read her mothers thoughts she would have already known about his pain-full sad eyes and how much he was hurting deep down inside. Instead she was experiencing them first hand, she could not understand why he had so much hate inside his sole and even though she had never judged him on what he had said up to now she herself was hurting inside for not being able to fully understand or even know, how to start taking some of the pain and hate away. She knew however that there wasn't a medicine to cure what was wrong inside him. In a sad voice Margaret found herself saying, you don't seem to have a very high opinion of your fellow man, do you feel the same way about me.

    Stepping towards her, the smile came back to his face. Don't take any notice of a grumpy old man, I have seen things that turned me this way, and stepping even closer, he ran his thumb down her cheek to the point of her chin and said. No one could hate a face and a mind as beautiful as yours, physically and mentally you are perfect, take it from one who knows.

With Her soft cheeks Blushing red she said, come on silly we are never going to get there, and linking his bad arm took off at a steady walk, she thought how warm a feeling his complimentary words gave her, she was always getting chatted up in the Swan but those words went in one ear and out the other, it was usually only the drink that gave them the courage anyway. But the further they walked the more she thought, this old man wasn't chatting her up, he was telling her the truth as he saw it and whatever he had wrong on the inside, he was lovely on the outside.

The path turned left over a little stone bridge that didn't have any water underneath and as the path narrowed with hawthorn bushes closing in on both sides she noticed from time to time, he would slow down and pick the head off a wild flower or the tips from the end of the hawthorn branches and put them inside his coat.

Do you press wild flowers she asked with curiosity?

No, they are for the wife.

The wife, Margaret replied with even more surprise than curiosity, does she press flowers.

No, she eats them.

She eats them, is she a vegetarian or something? Margaret had been well taken aback, and was tying to conjure up a picture in her mind of what a women might look like that would marry a man like him, not to mention the fact of where she was at this very moment, she had to be close because the flowers wouldn't last forever. Then it hit her, it was another Marx brothers joke.

Reading her face, Kevin stressed, they, are for the wife.

And For the first time Margaret felt a little twinge of jealousy as she replied you don't look like a married man.

With an unsurprised look he said. I don't. Tell me, what does a married man looks like these days.

Letting go of his arm, she turned and looked him in the face. Oh I don't know, you have seen some of what gets in the Swan, and if they are anything to go by you are perfectly normal.

But you aren't normal are you, and please I'm not trying to be cheeky, I cant put my finger on it, but its just that no matter how much you fit in with those people in the swan, you are still so much different. I know I've never met anyone like you in my whole life. And to be honest, if you are married, where is she.

She's close, Kevin said, but in some ways you have put your finger on it. We are not really married in the biblical sense.

What other way is there to be married, are you some kind of none religious sect that doesn't give vows to each other or has ten wives or something.

No it's closer to home than that, it's more of a mixed marriage kind of thing.

But most vicars nowadays will marry two people of different colours, I mean it doesn't happen around here because there aren't any coloured people, but I don't see the problem.

Tell me, Kevin said, were abouts are we heading, you know, that special place you were going to show me.

We are nearly there, this path goes straight on for miles but we are turning right just a few yards up and heading for those two tree covered hills.

Where the path divided they turned onto what was no more than a footpath of broken grass across an open field, and linking arm in arm they virtually doubled its width. The path was as straight as any roman would have made it, and it headed directly into the valley between the two hills. Not having given her an answer Margaret wasn't sure weather she had said too much and over stepped her mark but if she had, her silent companion hadn't shown her any sign of distaste. On reaching the edge of the valley Margaret pulled him off to the right and headed up the hill on another tiny pathway through the trees. If it hadn't have been for the path Margaret's silky smooth legs would have suffered severally. Between the thorns on the brambles and the spikes on the gorse her uncovered legs would have been a mass of scratches.

Chapter Eleven.
Margaret's, Secret View.

Reaching the top, Kevin found a small open grassy area were several unfortunate trees had been blown over in some great storm maybe twenty years previous.

From this high advantage point Margaret said. On a clear day she could see the whole world, and today was one of those days. In front of them the fields dropped away for over a mile and the ascended before dropping another mile and fading out on the shores of a flat calm sea. The Irish coast line seamed only a brisk walk away, were as far over to the south the thin sea mist covered outline of the isle of man sat like a small water surrounded island that could have come right out of the movie King Kong. The valley in front of them was spanned by a set of great man made arches that the railway had once used to transport coal, and the words (used to) meant what they said, for they were now a ruinous eye sore from a bygone age whose removal would have restored the valley to its former glory.

It's so quiet here now, but a hundred years or so ago, this place would have been a hive of industry. There must have been a none stop line of railway wagons ferrying coal down to the coast to fuel the steam ships. I love the quietness but I wonder were all the people went too that worked here, because if you think about it, there must have been hundreds.

Kevin had seen more of the world than most people, and looking at the young lady beside him, he thought, I wonder if she has ever been any further than ten miles from this very place, I wonder how far her imagination extends?

Then as if reading his mind, she said I would love to travel around the world and see the same places the people who worked here saw.

I don't think you would, Kevin said, and before she could ask why, he continued, they probably all died in the battle of the Somme or some other world war battle that some politician would put in the category of being Great.

Is that what you think happened to them, they all died.

He could see he had broken a dream and tried to reinstate it by saying, take no mind of me, I'm only guessing, I haven't any idea what happened to them, its just I always try when ever I can to knock the powers that be. And before you ask, it's the way the world has made me. Anyway you wanted to know about the wife and the pressed flowers. And Being a woman I bet you still do, am I right.

Margaret smiled and nodded at his perception.

Lets sit down here with our backs to this fallen tree and look out over this valley, the grass is soft and dry and as you say, from here we can see the world, and who knows from this advantage point we may be able to put some of the worlds problems to right. So the couple made them selves comfortable on this place Margaret called heaven and was probably the closest Kevin would ever get to the real thing. As I said, me and the wife or should I say the wife and I, could only be classed as none biblically married and believe you me theirs no holy person in the whole world would dare give us their blessing. So, young Margaret, I don't normally let anyone meet her, but as I said a little while ago, I know you to be a real lady, so I would like you to meet my little lady. Opening his coat slowly as not to scare her, Kevin said, Bun this is Margaret. Margaret, meet the wife. A little nose twitched as it took in the new smells that were coming first hand, and when Margaret spoke one long narrow ear lifted from its horizontal position on Buns back as if listening to what was being said.

Margaret's voice was one of relief, SHE`S your wife, now I understand what you were babbling on about, oh, I love rabbits can I hold her.

Well it isn't as simple as that, it would be if Bun thought she was a rabbit, but she doesn't. If I have a destiny, Bun must be part of it. I think it's a story worth listening to, so in those immortal words, are we all sitting comfortable, then I will begin.

Chapter Twelve.
Buns Story.

Bun has never known anyone but me from virtually the day she was born, it all started over two years ago when I arrived back from America with an invitation to stay at a friends castle in Scotland. I had been there about two weeks when on the day in question I was sitting on the lawn watching mine host, Big Andy McCready fly fishing on his lock to the rear of his castle, I remember it was the twentieth of July, because it was the day that changed my life. A voice came from behind us, shouting, Andy come and see what I've found. It was Andy's wife Helen who was returning from a walk with her two Alsatian dogs. The fingers of her left hand were cupped around something tiny and when she opened them, I saw for the first time the still body of what looked like a dead or dying newly born baby rabbit no bigger than a small mouse. The dogs chased a weasel from that rabbit set down near Foresters cottage; it was carrying this baby rabbit, but had to drop it to make its get away. What will I do with it she asked? A voice came back in the broadest Scottish accent there could ever be?

The wee beasties suffering, dunt it on the heed. The voice came from their gamekeeper a local wild life demolition expert who had just managed to put nine words together without a swear word mixed in. For him that was an accident, not an achievement. His name was Wee sweary Rab Smith. His nick name had been given to him, because of his management of the F word, and standing the height of a good sized mole hill in his grandfathers hob nailed boots and wearing three pairs of thick woollen socks to fill up the gaps, he wasn't classed as a giant. How he ever got to the position of game keeper I never did find out because even at the age of forty four, as he was then, he couldn't see or hear the length of his shot gun. Never the less I loved the man dearly, he had a heart of gold and there never was a task to big or small for him, mind you, he had to do it his way. But no matter that his mind was made up, that anything that was eatable was shot and eaten, normally in that order I watched him day after day in winter time, put food out for the little song birds and finches the same size as himself. I think the McCready's must have kept him because he always gave them one hundred an ten percent effort at all times whether, they wanted it or not. Anyway needless to say he didn't get his way, and Helen gave me the little parcel of lifeless energy. To me nothing is dead until its dead, and even then I gave what ever it was, time to be sure. I took Bun inside the castle and into the cookhouse, were I filled a hot water bottle with warm water, and putting her in a blanket laid her on top of it. Her neck had a small wound just below her ears and inside it I could see the biggest movement of her whole body, (maggots). They had just hatched and were tiny, and easily killed off with some antiseptic cream. Within an hour, the heat had put life back into her cold body, and the tiny Bun had put in her first bid for life. I made up a weak milk solution tinted with honey but her mouth was so small the only way I could get her to take any without drowning her was to put a drop on my wrist and let her lick it off. It was a great feeling when she did this because I knew it was her second and most important bid for life. For four weeks we went through the same thing every hour on the hour day and night, first feeding her then a sponge down with cotton wool to keep her clean. When she was ten days old I weighed her on cooks kitchen scales and Bun only came out at one and a half ounces, after that though she started to put on at least half an ounce every three days. If the cook ever found out what I was doing with her scales she would have hit the high notes and I would have been for the high jump. But I had to use them, because as long as she was putting weight on, I knew she going forward and doing ok. The longer she lived the more energy I seemed to get, I had seen so many living things die in my lifetime that to see Bun live was a refreshing experience. She took my mind away from my own problems with concentrating on hers, there wasn't a hour went by that I didn't start kissing her on her nose and continued kissing her up over her head and down the back of her neck and every time I would say, come on baby you can make it, your going to live. The first time her eyes opened, I asked her what she could see, not that she could answer, but that didn't matter, I talked anyway. I talked and talked and talked, and I think it must have helped in some way because now we seem to be on the same wavelength and she understands everything I say. It was four weeks before she started to eat greens, and she started off with clover stalks, the flowers were to big and once she got to them she nipped them off and they fell on my nee, I was so proud of her, but by this time I realised she wasn't going to be a normal rabbit, or have a normal life. Her balance was all wrong, I think it was probably from her inner ear being damaged by the maggots plus she didn't have full coordination with one of her back legs. I think that was due to the damage done to her spinal cord when the weasel attacked and thought it had paralysed her ready to be carried away and eaten for tea. Fortunately for Bun the dogs upset the weasels plan. Life got so much easier when she was four weeks old because at night time she slept in my arm pit or what she really liked was under my chin, I didn't get much sleep because I was frightened I might move and squash her, but I didn't have the pressure of feeding her because a handful of clover stalks kept her going all night. My biggest problem was keeping a nappy on her, she was to young to know not to pee in bed and there were also the rabbit dottles if the nappy came off I ended up having what looked like tiny pepper corns stuck all over my body and I mean all over. When I look back I don't know how she survived.

    Margaret broke into his worded thoughts, saying I think it must have been pure dedication; there isn't anyone I know that would have put him or herself through so much that took up so much time, just for a rabbit.

    What's time anyway, mind you I thought at first it would only have been a matter of a few weeks, eight, maybe twelve at the most, and now two years later I wouldn't be parted from her for a second, she shows me so much love. Most nights she won't go to sleep until she has washed my eyes with her tongue.

I don't know how, but I know everything she wants just by the look on her face or the way she moves. And She must have learned the English language because she responds to what ever I say to her. It may sound stupid or nonsense but we talk the whole time and even though there's not a word can come from her lips, she answers me every time. Once she had survived eight weeks the pressure was totally off me, see could eat anything and she was house trained, apart from bouts of dizziness and not been able to walk proper she could hold her own. I came back from America with a job to do, one I promised my family and my self and two years down the line I still haven't got it done, but as I said before what is time anyway. Bun has been so good for me, I'm not sure if my wife didn't send her to look after me, and not the other way around. If I believed in reincarnation I would have said that Bun was the reincarnation of my wife. If destiny has anything to do with anything, I'm not sure how long I would last without her, or the trouble I would get into. She is probably the calm before the storm, and it would be some storm.

Forgive me if I am wrong, but you've mentioned your wife a few times, and it sounds, as though she died, was it an accident or an illness.

Kevin spouted out, MURDERED was the word I would have used, then thinking the better of his blunt outcry, said sorry, I didn't mean to take it out on you.

Murdered, I'm sorry I didn't mean to pry, Margaret saw a single tear leave a watery eye and pulled by gravity over his cheek slowly disappear into a mass of blond whiskers. A picture was forming in her head; things he had said that she hadn't understood at the time were starting to make sense. His hatred of his fellow man now had an understanding ear.

She repeated to the now silent old man, I'm so sorry, as you said before, women ask to many questions.

Turning to face her she could see the tell tale sign of a

matching tear trail on his other cheek. He spoke not in a loud angry voice but one of a beaten man with no hope left in the world. Its nothing for you to worry about, Janet was my world, you only asked a polite question, to which I gave a rude answer, if anyone should say sorry its me. And, I am sorry, so if you have anything you want to know, just go ahead and ask.

Margaret had the feeling, he wanted to talk, but she had questions she didn't like to ask. So being as diplomatic as she could, said, tell you what, why don't you tell me what happened I'm a good listener and talking does help.

Showing the distortion of pain on his sad face he looked down at Bun as if asking for guidance. Then Lifting her out of her pocket, he held her warm furry body against his cheek and kissed her on the side of her face, were upon Bun turned her head and licked the dieing, drying. Tear trail, that a few moments previous had been a moving motion of emotion. There wasn't time to think If Buns actions or her words had been the catalyst, for without warning the old man burst into tears, the floods of pent up emotion burst the banks of time, his whole body shook as if it had been attached to some road workers Jack Hammer.

Margaret jumped up from her sitting position and knelt down before him, cradling his head under her chin with her arms, she had never seen a child cry so helplessly before never mind a grown man. What would her mother do in a situation like this, if only she had been there to ask? The only thing Margaret could think of to say, was get it out of your system, you'll feel better then. It was a good five minuets before she felt the sobbing start to subside, and five minuets may only have been a short time in life, but it had meant ten years of torture for the old man she was holding. As he seamed to be gathering his composure, Margaret lent back and kissed him on the forehead, only to see that Bun was washing his face from underneath.

Do you feel any better she asked, her voice filled with compassion.

A little, for the time being anyway, It comes and goes, its

happened before so its probably going to happen again, its not very manly of me is it.

Rubbish, Margaret said, men have feelings as well, well they do except when it comes to overcoming shyness and asking a girl out.

Kevin laughed; I can't believe there isn't a man in this village hasn't asked you out.

Oh theirs plenty done that, but after Mum has interrogated them, they do a runner. Mum never did want me marrying any lad from the village; she always said marry a rich man from as far away as possible. I bet Mum wished she had kept quiet now, because no one ever came close to asking me to marry them now.

And it would have been nice to be asked. Kevin said anticipating her next sentence.

Exactly, replied Margaret.

Well, if I had been a hundred years younger, I wouldn't have taken no for an answer, mind you I think your mother would scare me a little.

Hoping it would make him feel better she smiled and said, Never mind mum, if you had been fifteen years younger I might have said yes.

You just might eh, and pigs would fly.

Bursting into fits of laughter at the silliness of their conversation they both lent forward as if reading each other's thoughts and gave each other a quick gentle kiss then started to laugh again.

Kevin went a little quiet, then Without warning started to tell his story, he wasn't looking at Margaret who was now sitting cross legged in front of him, he just seemed to be staring straight through her, across the valley and across the sea, in fact he looked as though he was staring at a place so far away it could have been one inch behind him. But no matter were it was she didn't think he would ever reach it.

Chapter thirteen. Janet's Story.

Janet was so tiny, she used to say she was five foot, but she would have been lucky to make four foot ten in high heels. I met her by accident, if you can do such a thing, when I was eighteen and just out of cadetship.

In those days a police constable could be transferred to anywhere but his hometown and I had been sent to a small mining town that had a rugby league team on every street. I never saw so many broken noses in one place in my life, it had the hardest but fairest men I ever met. In those days, no one had any money, and you joined a rugby team for the friendship, a free hot bath and the biggest tattie pot you ever saw.

As Kevin spoke, Margaret noticed how gentle he subconsciously stroked Buns ears and body and if he stopped for a second Bun would wash his hand, and then when she stopped, Kevin would start all over again.

I was on duty one hot day, just doing a walk around the town and I heard the bell and cry of an ice cream vender. So following his sound, I found him in the next street with a little group of hopeful kids hanging about. Nowadays we have proper ice cream vans, but in those days, all the salesman had was a three-wheeled pushbike with a chest freezer stuck between the two front wheels. This one had the name, Hartley's Ice's in big black letters on the sides of the freezer. When I got there, a little girl was in front of me; at least I thought she was a little girl. She asked for two, tuppeny cornets, but then changed her mind and asked for one tuppeny one and two penny ones which she handed to two small kids beside her. She then walked away to her front door with the one cornet.

The sales man whispered she does that every time, if those kids are watching she will give them her ice cream and keep the one for her mother. Before I knew it, he had told me everything he knew about her, how her father had died in the first world war without ever seeing her born, then her mother caught some heritable illness that is passed down to only women when they give birth to a girl, and Janet had never married, giving all her time to her long ailing and deteriorating mother. Yes, Janet was more than old enough to be married, I found it so hard to believe, in fact she was all of four years older than myself, Twenty two, I wouldn't have said she looked more than a young fourteen. I turned and watched her open the garden gate and walk up the path to the front door. Looking at her now as an adult and not a child I couldn't help but notice what a lovely bum she seemed to have under her clean but tight worn out trousers.

That night, I couldn't sleep for thinking about her, my body was a mass of tingly electric shocks, and my mind refused to close down. The next day was even worse; I couldn't get her from my mind. The next seven days seamed to take a whole year in slow motion. Every day I walked the same beat past her home but never saw her the once, I even walked it on my day off.

A week went by and we all ended up in front of the same ice cream man only this time there were four kids, I made sure Janet had got there first, and when she asked the sales man if he could split a tuppeny cornet four ways. I could see he was about to shake his head, so I mouthed to him over her head that I would pay the difference. I stood in silence as I watched her go through the very same motions as the week before, and then disappear behind their front door still wearing what appeared to be the same clothes only by now they were looking a little bit grubbier.

I paid and accepted my ice cream cornet without a word leaving my lips, but I did say to myself it didn't taste anywhere near as good as the week before. The following week went by just like the previous one, a sleepless nightmare, I didn't know what was wrong with me, except I couldn't keep this girl out of my mind for a second, so I made it my job to be there at the same time and place and hoped the kids hadn't doubled in quantity again. This time there not only wasn't any kids, there wasn't a Janet. And For the first time in my life I found myself feeling so disappointed. I could have screamed I was desperate to see a girl that didn't even know I existed. That night, I sat down and gave myself a talking to, but it made no difference I was convinced that if God did make the world in six says, he didn't have a day of rest on the seventh like his book says, because on that day he created Janet. The following week was the same, no Janet, and no kids. The vender must have noticed me watching her house because he said, if I was looking for Janet, it might be a while before we see her. He had heard they were very short of money and her mother had been more ill than normal.

I asked him if he was sure they were in the house.

He said of coarse they are, they haven't the money to go any were else.

My mind was made up in a second, I said give me two big cornets for the ladies.

For Janet and her mother the vender replied, if it's for them lets make them extra big for the same price.

I never thought of my self as the bold type, but knowing Janet as I had for all of two minuets in the last three weeks, I had to get her either in or out of my system once and for all. I said to Mr Hartley, as I paid for the cornets. You can't fly the flag if you don't pull the rope. By the look on his face, I gathered he hadn't grasped what I was meaning, but being honest with myself, I must have had the same look, because I wasn't quite sure what I meant. Watched by Mr Hartley, I took my peace of mind and goodwill offering along with the sickest feeling I had ever had in my stomach, up the path and knocked on the door. I don't know what or who I was expecting to answer, or whether I was hoping no one would, but as it was, it was Janet that answered, and even though I got a bit tongue tied I managed to splutter out that I'd heard her mother was sick and thought she might like an ice cream. It was a lie but it was also the truth, anyway, I met Janet face to face for the first time, my first impression was, she would look tremendous in tight jeans and a baggy matching long woolly jumper. Her red hair went straight to her shoulders without a curl or a wave of any kind. She had a Childs figure, and as I found out later, if I put my hands on her waist I could touch my fingers making a complete circle. Janet let me into a house of clean nothingness and sitting by a small coal fire in an old battered brown leather armchair covered by an even older patchwork quilt for extra warmth was her mother. I had never seen anything living that looked so frail. I was sure the ice cream would only make her feel colder, I wasn't even sure she should have it, but Janet's mother insisted. She had a tiny weak voice that sounded as though could fade away at any second. I found out later that ice cream and porridge were about the only two things she could keep down. The house was clean but for the love of me there was nothing in it, they couldn't have been any wealthier than Ada. Janet didn't look embarrassed at their situation, I think for all the world she had seen; she probably thought the way they lived was normal. She told me quietly that she had to hand feed her mother and placing the cornets in a bowl, thanked me. I told her mum to keep warm and Janet walked me to the door. I didn't want to sound insensitive or out of order, but as we parted company on the doorstep I turned and heard myself saying, do you fancy taking me out somewhere sometime. Janet in her sweetest manner said, I can't afford to.

My heart was broken. Here was a young lady going no were fast, who had less than nothing, but would spend her last penny to buy someone else's child an ice cream. And the only thing she had going for her was the sexiest bum I had ever seen. I thought for a second, and then gathering all my strength together, found myself saying, would you let me pay if I ask you to marry me. Looking back, I don't know if I simply felt sorry for their whole situation and just wanted to do something to help, or it was love at first sight. But for whatever reason I had at the time, they were the only words that wanted to come out. Anyway Janet blushed bright red and closed the door without saying a word. I walked down the path calling myself all the dummies under the sun, not that I regretted what I had asked her, I didn't, but what was she supposed to say in reply, how could she answer a question that I didn't know I was going to ask in the first place. Mentally kicking myself, I walked out onto the pavement and far off in the distance I heard a voice that broke my train of thought and brought me back to reality.

How was the old lass. The voice answered it self by saying, not to good by the look on your face.

You were right I said, their whole situations not to good, and I didn't make it any better.

You didn't, how could an ice cream hurt.

The ice cream was fine, its just me, I talk to much, anyway see you next week if the force don't transfer me some were else first, come to think of it, maybe it would be better if I applied for a transfer, it would be one way of clearing my head. The next day I wanted to give Janet's house as wide a birth as possible, but it was on my beat so unless their was a bank robbery or something taking me else were, I had to walk by, and it was just as well I did. As I approached Janet's house I tried not to look, but couldn't help myself. I felt my heart flutter as I was sure a living room curtain moved, then as I came level with the gate the front door opened and an arm along with a quiet voice beckoned me in. Removing my helmet I entered the house to find Janet standing behind the door shaking like a leaf and looking red faced. She was finding it hard to get words of any kind to leave her tiny lips, but when she did they weren't what I expected.

My mother would like a word with you young man, and still shaking pointed in the direction of were her mother had been the day before.

The little old lady watched me walk towards her, she was trying to smile and I could see she wanted to, but she was at the stage were even a smile made her body hurt, She was on the edge of giving in to two decades of pain that had made a forty something year old look twice her age. I didn't realise it at that moment, but I was to be her relief that would finally give her the choice to let go. Janet handed me a little wooden three-legged milking stool and I stood it on the floorboards as close to her mother as I could get.

Sit down young man, Janet said in a formal but more relaxed tone.

Don't be so formal; the old lady said reprimanding her own daughter's words. Yesterday you asked Janet to marry you, I was wondering why, when you don't even know her.

I have asked myself the same question over and over again, and you are right, until yesterday we had never even talked. Apart from standing next to Janet when she bought ice cream from Mr Hartley we have never had any contact. The only way I can explain it, is, since the first day I saw Janet I felt as though I was like catching the cold, my body started tingling all over, I cant sleep, I couldn't concentrate on anything but her, and when I came in here and saw how ill you where I felt so sorry for you both I just wanted to look after you'se any way I could.

Janet's mother looked me in the eye and said, and now you regret your impetuousness.

Only the embarrassment I've caused your family, I didn't mean to hurt either of your feelings, never mind the fact that Janet probably cant stand the sight of me. I'm not very good at talking to ladies on a friendly basis I've never had much experience at it.

Mr Hartley came in after you left and told us it was your idea about the ice cream, she lent painfully forward and rested her wrinkled hand on mine, you sound to honest for a police man, but then you are still very young.

Janet scolded her mother in a nice sort of way saying, Mother you can't say that, every one isn't the same.

At my time of life I can say what I like, especially if I believe it to be true, it may be that this young man will prove me wrong, he's painfully young just as I am painfully old but if I am any judge of character he's good husband material and looking at Janet, she said, I have nothing against him coming to take you courting.

I first looked at Janet, whose face was crimson, then back at her mother. Look misses. Then it hit me, I didn't know their second name or Janet's mothers first for that matter. Sorry I don't think we have been properly introduced yet. Looking at Janet, I said my names Kevin Hodgson.

Taking my cue, Janet said, this is my mother, Martha Brown.

Look Janet's mum, before we go any further, a lot, in fact everything depends on Janet, I don't want her to jump into anything she doesn't want to, or being pushed into. I had no intention of getting married, but if I did, it has to be to a girl that loves me, and not just for the sake of it, and definitely not if Janet thinks she could never have any feelings for me.

Don't worry; no one is pushing anyone into anything. We talked about it all last night and Janet may have been taken very much by surprise but she never would do anything she didn't want to. And for your own piece of mind it was her that asked me to talk to you.

To be honest, I was well surprised Janet had seen the same attraction in me. We got married six months later just before her mother died, it pleased old Martha no end to see us happily married, and we both knew it gave her the strength to die. It was a sad time for us all but it was also a relief that it was the end of her pain. Once we were married we got a modern police house to live in that made life a lot easier. Janet must have been the shyest person in the world, she got embarrassed at the least thing, and she never ever changed, I think it must have been the way she was brought up, never having contact with many people. I liked to sleep with no clothes on, especially in the summer, but she made me wear pyjamas all the time. She would never get undressed with the light on, and if I teased her by saying I was going to turn on the light half way through her undressing, she would jump under the covers to finish off, we never stopped cuddling each other or laughing for that matter. Janet always insisted we fall asleep with my arms around her, I didn't have to be asked because I could never get enough of her and also I was sure it made her feel safe and wanted. I think she always thought she was going to spend her life alone when her mother died and this was her way of making sure I was still there.

Our only setback was if we should try for children, with the hereditary health problem if Janet had a girl. But we were lucky because our first child was a boy and even though we both desperately wanted more, I decided to call it a day. I wouldn't take the chance of the same thing happening to Janet as it did her mother, though sometimes with hindsight I do regret my decision.

Margaret had sat silent, waiting for Kevin to come up for air, at what seamed a break in the one-way conversation she stepped in.

Do you ever see your son on your travels? She realised before she had finished her sentence that something was amiss, it may have been the look in his eye or the tenseness of his body, but what ever it was Margaret knew she had hit a nerve.

Kevin looked at Margaret then let his gaze drift over her shoulder, his hand was fondling Buns ears, as glassy eyed he started again. Our lad disappeared along with our granddaughter ten years ago, I pushed the men that did it, and that's how I ended up like this. Lifting his right arm he gestured, wiggling what was left of the leather thong covered hand. To my shame that was the one time I could do nothing to make Janet safe, she died at their hands without dignity or mercy of any kind. Their mistake was leaving me alive, I never was a religious man to start with, but the three that did it will find out one day the meaning of the phrase, an eye for an eye.

There was fiery water in the eyes of Margaret as she said, all this happened ten years ago, were they never brought to justice.

Justice never managed to catch up with them, it didn't even get close, and they made sure of that. The way I look at it is, justice can take various forms, and my justice will be justice when the time is right.

Chapter Fourteen. Gung Fu

When will that be Margaret queried.

Well it would have been two years ago but this big long eared rat on my knee put a hold on my intentions.

Margaret had more than a good idea what he intended doing would never be classed as legal. What if you get into trouble it would be you who went to prison.

Exactly, I would be the first person they would look for, but the thought of prison doesn't really bother me, because the way I look at it, I am already serving a life sentence. My problem is, they don't take rabbits, so what would happen to her. She is the life and soul of my party, so I have to think of her first and that's the way it will stay until fate lends a hand. In the mean time I have my Gung Fu to help me stay as fit as I can, and one day who knows.

What's Gung Fu? Margaret asked, then continued, by stating, is it some kind of health food.

In a way yes, but not the way you think. Its more of a health food for the mind than the body. Once my external injuries got better I took up Karate, you know, self defence, unarmed combat, and I got good at it. What I lacked in skill I made up with aggression, it wasn't hard, I just got it into my head that any opponent was Mister nasty. The piece of scum that executed, and destroyed my dreams, and my whole world. Karate was good; it was the start of getting me fit physically. But I found the art to soft and on the defensive with any contact being none contact, if you can follow what I mean.

Margaret was a little lost but nodded in agreement.

Kevin continued. I tried every kind of self-defence but always came back to Karate Then something changed my life, you know when destiny steps in and gives you a push. I got picked to fight for Great Britain in the world Karate championships in Japan. Oh, I was over the moon, until I found out how much it cost. There was no way I could afford it on my pension. I even thought about just getting there and thumbing my way back, but how do you thumb it from Japan, anyway it didn't matter because with the money I had I would have had to thumb it there, never mind back. I started to get depressed, until good old destiny stepped in again with all the people of my local town clubbing together not only to pay for my trip but to give me a good time as well. The trip did me the power of good I loved every second. The way of life over there was so different and to my surprise I didn't find the opposition any harder, oh they were good but they must have been only fighting for a trophy or the honour of being number one. Were as, I was fighting for a totally different reason and not one, that any of them would understand.

Watching the bouts I only saw one man that I thought would give me trouble. He was a Chinese American and I wanted so much to be put in against him. My only objection was to his size; I would still have felt dishonourable hitting someone so tiny and weighing in at no more than eight stone. Not that it should have bothered me because he went through opponents just as fast as I did. He was so fast with his moves but even with the perfect body he had I couldn't understand were he got his power from, he was super natural. The one thing I did like about him was he had a style all his own, he had ten moves to everyone else's one, I didn't know whether it was because of his speed or what but he didn't do the regular Karate moves, most times he was so fast you couldn't see what moves he was doing. I was desperate to fight him just to try and learn something because I figured his style was what I had been looking for. Anyway it wasn't to be because as I said the sport was one of not drawing blood, but I kept doing the opposite and ended up getting disqualified in the semi finals.

The little Chinese guy won his semi and then took the winners trophy and I thought that was that, until I left for the airport, were Destiny stepped in again. I wasn't far from boarding the plane home, when a student of the Chinese American Winner said his master was offering me a place in his American school of Gung Fu all expenses paid. And that's what I did, I ended up in

Seattle where I met the owner face to face and let me tell you, it wouldn't have mattered how force full I had been at the contest, I would never have been ready for him, in real life this little man could run up the wall of a room and stick to the ceiling before running down the other side, he defied gravity, he defied logic, he was phenomenal, he had an aurora that surrounded his body and his personality that was electrifying. His defence was anything and everything, kicks, head buts, even fingers in the eyes, his philosophy was, hurt rather than be hurt, maim rather than be maimed, and kill rather than be killed. He changed the way I looked at things, their was none of our British stiff upper lip and fair play or feeling a coward by getting in a sly dig, his way, was one of self preservation, if someone attacked you with criminal intent then he lost any rights he may ever have had, and gave you the right to the freedom to use anything in your power to stop him. I thought I was good, until the first time I faced him in mock combat. He told me I was standing all wrong and there for off balance. He told me to strike him anywhere I wanted, we were surrounded by maybe twenty of his students and I thought he was just being smart and trying to show me up so I went for him lock stock and barrel without warning. I never saw what hit me, and I was hit three times before I hit the ground. He picked me up knowing I had learned my first lesson, a lesson his students already knew. There was no man in the world more deadly than he. After dismissing his class we sat down to the evening meal his wife had prepared, I may have not said but I was staying with the Lee family and his training area was also his living room, in fact it was nearly his whole house. He may have been a great man but he didn't live great, and I remember thinking, I was going to have to get a job to at least pay for the food I was eating.

    As we sat eating, I asked Master Lee why he had asked me to stay with him if I was so easy to beat.

    He continued my sentence, saying, because you thought you were unbeatable and I have to make sure you are before you go back to England. I know what is pushing you, my sister died a similar death as your wife and there would be no justice in you not being able to fulfil your wishes, there for it is my wish to help you fulfil your wish.

I was taken aback that he knew my story and asked him how he knew.

There is no mystery, I saw you fighting with more force than your body allowed and knew there had to be a reason. For a man to be able to do something nature wasn't supposed to allow him to do, the reason had to be one of the deepest pain and I thought I recognised that pain. It wasn't hard to find out the truth from your colleges. But if you want to take out the powers of darkness from your enemies, then first you have to look at them through more than the eyes you see with.

I wasn't sure I understood much, if anything he said, but for the love of me he had my attention, I was spell bound.

Master Lee continued, You are not of my race, there for there is much you will not understand or even believe, it will be hard to find out the truth, it will be even harder for you to believe the truth when you see it. Before you can see or believe in anything, I have to be able to get you to believe in yourself.

I do believe in myself I said a little indignant.

Master Lee looked at me shaking his head and said if that was so, how was it that it was you and not I who lay on the ground at our first session today.

In truth, I could not say I wasn't ready for him because I had made the first move, my only excuse was the truth, he was better than me, and that was what I told him.

Master Lee told me that my answer was very true, but not necessarily for the reasons I thought. The difference between all men is slight a large man can be more powerful but slow were as a small man like myself should be the opposite.

I butted in, except that doesn't really count, with training man can make his body the perfect fighting machine, it doesn't matter whether you are big or small, look at yourself, the muscles on your body look like they were moulded out of steel, you must have spent years training to get them like that, no wonder you are so powerful.

Having waited until I had finished talking which was the polite Chinese way, and not butting in like the totally opposite English version. Master Lee said you are right again, but you are also wrong. A man or woman can do all the things you say if they train their body, but I am not talking about your body, I am talking about your mind, to achieve all the power of the universe we have to train your mind to believe in itself, to believe it can do all the things nature gives away free. I teach students of all races, each one is different; therefore I teach my style of Gung Fu, to each one of them differently, even though it looks as though I am teaching them collectively. Because of my birth sign, as a newborn baby, I was taken to a Shaolin temple and placed in the care of Shaolin Monks to be taught in all their ways and beliefs. My former masters frown upon what I teach my students, because we are not allowed to give away the secrets of Shaolin to people of other races. The way I look at it is, I am only teaching self-defence to my style, not Shaolin, but in your case it will be different, I believe your quest will end up in self-destruction if I do not help. Destiny as you call it has brought us together, and if you can recognise it when it happens then destiny can change the path you walk. Without this knowledge most people walk the same path all their lives until they have walked too far. We can help destiny to help us, but first you have to be able to see with your mind what you are not looking for with your eyes. I will teach your mind in the private secrecy of my home and your body will be taught at my normal classes, by the time you are ready to leave for England you will be able to walk on water, defy gravity and not be seen by the naked eye. I will give you all the powers that Shaolin posses. Remember this at all times, the inner mind can make you the most powerful man in the Universe, or it can make you the weakest. Once you believe in yourself, all the powers of the Universe start to surround you and protect you, but the second you stop believing they start to leave. You must be like a magnet, drawing in all metal objects, each object gives you more knowledge, and knowledge is power. I am your magnetism, I believe it is my destiny to magnetise you with knowledge.

And that's what happened, I stayed in Seattle for several years until Master Lee was happy with me, we parted when he and his family had to go back to Hong Kong. I could have went with them but I decided to stay on in America for some time longer and teach the Gung Fu style to any one interested including the police force, who nick named me the real Lone Ranger, that's all there was to it, the rest I think you know.

Margaret had been subconsciously stroking Bun as she sat their spell bound in his story and waited like a polite man from China to ask her first question. Do you believe it was destiny, us meeting like we did, and if it was what path do we take now.

Kevin wasn't sure how Margaret had meant her questions, the expression on her face and the softness of her voice to him had hidden depths to the words that had come from her lips.

What path do we take now he repeated, how about the one we came, your mum will be getting a little worried, its going to be late by the time we get back.

Margaret looking at her wristwatch forgot her question saying Gosh, look at the time.

Kevin was about to put Bun back inside his coat when Margaret asked if she could hold her before they left.

It isn't as easy as that, stroking her is one thing, but putting your hands around her is another, she can bite and scratch, I don't normally let anyone hold her but seeing its you, just pick her up gently and let her sit on your knee but whatever happens don't drop her.

Margaret did what Kevin said and followed his instructions on how to lift her, using one hand under Buns chest and the other under her bum, and never lifting a rabbit by the ears. Bun didn't seem to object, but after a second Margaret cried out, oh no.

What's wrong Kevin said fearing the worst, has she bit

you?

No, worse than that, she's peed on me.

Kevin had to subdue his smile, sorry I forgot about that one but at least she likes you, its her way of saying she doesn't want to be with you without hurting you.

Margaret lifted her wet trouser skirt from her legs and said, we'll have to go home, now, and gosh rabbit pee stinks doesn't it.

That's why dogs find them so easy, rabbit pee is a dead give away with the emphasis on the word dead. Before we go I better give Bun a stretch, if theirs one thing she likes it's a stretch. So taking her back Kevin placed her on the grass with her head pointing away from him, then running his hand and stump down either side of her, he stopped when he got to her tiny waist. This seemed to be the signal for her to stretch, and balanced in Kevin's safe grip, she stretched out full stretch with her front and back legs together yawning at the same time. Bun stayed there for a second as Kevin massaged her waist and back in what seemed a well organised commonplace ritual. As soon as the massage stopped Bun gathered her body back together and waited for the every day lift to her inside pocket home.

Retracing their steps Margaret found herself wishing the return journey twice as long, each step was taking her one step closer to losing the individual attention she was getting with her captivating male companion. He had never answered her question on destiny, and she was intelligent enough to realise he had skirted around it on purpose, but all the same it had just made her think all the harder. Was there a reason for them meeting as they had, was there a reason to the fact that she had never married, or even come close to it. Boy friends her own age always wanted to marry, but the closer they tried to get, the further away they became. In her whole life she had never been as content as she was with this old man who she hadn't known but half a day, it felt as though something she had been waiting years for had finally arrived. Margaret knew, what she was thinking was true. He had a nice smile and an easy gentle nature; his manner was one of complete tranquillity the day after the storm. His inner and outer calmness seemed to reflect all that was good in the world. Of coarse he was older than her, but he wasn't as old as her mum or dad, and what would people say, what would her mum say, nearly speaking her thoughts out aloud at the shock of the idea, Margaret said to herself, quite a lot knowing mum. Had he been more presentable, with nicer clothes and a haircut or two he probably would look more down to earth, and not as noticeable. Still linking his arm she wondered what he would really look like with all his whiskers and hair cut down to civilian normality, not that she could ever see this man as a normal civilian. Her thoughts were only just out of her head, when Kevin said.

Is there anyone in the village cuts hair, I think its time I got this thatch off.

More than pleased to have another chance to be close to him, Margaret couldn't wait to say, I can do that no problem, I do mum and dads and theirs always turns out ok.

Well it doesn't have to be fancy, only shorter, I had thought of a Yule Brinner but maybe that would be a bit drastic.

I'll cut it to suit your face, that is once I can see your face, laughing at her own joke Margaret said, tell me, what made you say those big trees at the hall were planted by man and didn't just plant themselves.

His reply was not what she expected, not that she had any idea what to expect.

I don't suppose you would believe me if I told you, but they told me so.

At her blank expression he said. I better give you a more logical answer. Wild trees never grow in straight lines and all the same size, they grow to the shape of the wind and the sun. Man, is the only thing that plants in straight rows.

Margaret just nodded, her expression to logic was one of acceptance as the now, very close but still odd couple linked their way home retracing their steps virtually to the foot print. If any one had followed them, they would have heard nothing but laughs and continues jovial banter, more reminiscent of young lovers in their teens, than the age they were. Closed to the public, the Swans front door was now locked as the couple entered the main street. There was little movement even for a Friday except the stationary ladder was now in full employment, as its owner, Father Eric Holm busied himself in his art of cleaning windows.

    An s shaped hook held his bucket of warm soapy water about the third rung down as Father Eric worked like a man with six arms, a chamois leather in one and a wet cloth in the others to make up for the time lost due to his miss spent morning.

Father Eric was one man who knew what every one had in their rooms, up stairs and down, front and back, because it was his job to look threw windows. He unknowingly helped ladies get on with their house work, because no self respecting house wife wanted any one to see an untidy room, and if Father Eric was doing his rounds it meant they had to get a move on and get cleaned up before he reached them. The oncoming couple went unnoticed as Father Eric's arms and lips moved at the same time, even though he was deep in conversation with someone on the other side of the glass, it didn't stop him from working. Passing underneath him, Father Eric could be heard saying, its ok love, I'll make sure I get right in the corners.

    We will have to go around the back because I didn't bring my key and just in case mum has locked the side yard loading door, lets pop down Johnny's Ally, it's the quickest way.

    Kevin said Old Johnny must still make fish and chips if the smell is anything to go by.

    As they entered the three-foot wide ally they found themselves dwarfed by the gable ends of two houses almost back to back. Kevin was a little shocked to find Old Johnny was still the proprietor. And said Old Johnny was an old man when I was last here, or maybe he just looked old. When you are in your teens, any one ten years older was ancient. I can remember kids bringing in old news papers and empty jam jars, and Johnny would swap them for a bag of chips with scrapings, the kids always asked for scrapings. You know, the bits of cooked batter that had fallen off the fish; I think they liked them better than the chips.

Entering the Swan's rear yard Kevin found himself facing a large square grass lawn cut to within half an inch, with a three-foot concrete path surrounding it and an eight-foot wall surrounding them on four sides. On top of the walls were the cemented remains of broken glass bottles that reflected their various colours in the late noon sun. Once passed the grass lawn, Margaret opened another yard door that led them to a concreted walled yard holding the outside toilets and the side-loading door.

As they entered the back kitchen her mum smiled as if unconcerned and asked, had a good time, if I knew you were going to be so long I would have made you a picnic.

Dad back from work yet mum.

Ye, and he's a sleep so don't make to much noise, I didn't tell him who you were with, because you know what he's like. No offence meant Mister Hodgson but you do look a bit like Nan nook of the north.

Thank you Misses Bryan, Nan nook was a great warrior and explorer. I am honoured to be mistaken for him.

Peggy smiled and said, that wasn't exactly what I meant.

Margaret laughed out aloud saying its ok Mum, I'm going to remedy your worries, Kevin, is going to let me cut his hair.

Peggy smiled and said, got a death wish, have you Kevin. OH and another thing, we have big mousetraps down, so if that furry rodent of yours goes walk abouts in the middle of the night, it's not my fault.

You heard about Bun then mum.

Bun is it, it seems like you are on first names with every one, I don't suppose there is anything else I haven't been told, like you are going to elope to Gretna Green and Bun is best man.

Margaret blushed a little at the closeness of her mothers

joke or perception, then regained her composure by replying, best women mum, Bun is a lady in every respect of the word.

Peggy sniffed and said, our Margaret I don't care much for the perfume you are wearing.

Oh that was Bun, she peed on me.

Peggy laughed and said, some lady, if she peed on you, and while we are on the subject what happens through night, I mean is she housetrained.

Bun is fully house trained, misses Bryan, but if she does need to go she will tell me well in advance of anything arriving.

Well just in case she has to go, the back door and garden key will be in that draw there, and pointed at the second draw to the right of the back door.

You are very trusting Misses Bryan, especially when you don't know me. I mean I could rob the place and take off.

You could rob the place and take off without the keys, but you wont. I trusted you the first time I spoke to you, and after finding out who you really were from P C Shaw and P C Park I don't think I would mind if you did run away with our Margaret to Gretna Green. Oh and another thing, my names Peggy and my husband when he wakes up is Tom. And our Margaret, you can cut Kevin's hair in the yard. If I had known you were going to cut it we could have had a few bets on what it would weigh. Then added, for charity of coarse. And Margaret, go and change that stinky dress before half the dogs in the village decide to eat you.

When Margaret slipped upstairs to change, Peggy pulled Kevin into the bar, and talking quietly said, I knew you were hurting from the second I talked to you, does Margaret know everything about you.

No, there was no need for her young ears to hear all the bad bits, anyway we will be gone tomorrow or the day after.

Peggy was about to say, we, when she remembered Bun, and instead said, oh ye, I see, but what about Margaret, you do know she's got a crush on you.

Yes I do, I saw it coming, and don't get me wrong she's a

lovely lass and any man would be proud to have her by his side, but I haven't encouraged her, or am I likely to, my time is spoken for and to be honest Misses Bryan I don't need the responsibility any more. If you do know my whole story then I'm sure you can understand why.

Sure I do, but I know my daughter and I don't want her hurt. I know you wouldn't hurt her on purpose, but pretending nothings happening wont make her feelings go away, if you have to leave, please say something to her, give her a bit of warning. Peggy looked away towards the window for a second. Her eyes glazed as if deep in thought, seeking an answer that wasn't there to be found. Then again, maybe you are right, pretending nothing has happened would be for the best. Margaret's footsteps could be heard returning down the old wooden stairs. So Peggy grabbed Kevin's arm and pulling him back through to the kitchen saying, please don't tell her I said anything to you.

Misses Bryan the thought never entered my head.

No more words were spoken as Margaret came in holding a comb and a pair of scissors and dressed in blue jeans and a blue baggy woollen top. Kevin recognised the outfit and the hidden meaning, but didn't let on or make a comment, he just continued his little game of pretending.

What's with the silence, been talking about me have you.

Only how I might have shorter ears after you've finished.

Margaret pulled out an old cotton sheet from the cupboard and told Kevin to bring the kitchen stool with him outside into the yard. Once outside he took off his coat and hung it on the latch of the yard door, then at Margaret's request sat on the stool, were upon he and Bun were covered with the cotton sheet.

And what style would sir like today giggled Margaret. But before he could answer she continued, your head looks like a giant candyfloss sticking out of this sheet.

Just give me a short back and sides with a crew cut on the top and if that turns out ok I wont need to run away and hide, mind you once you have finished I wouldn't mind that bath and a shave just to get tided up for tonight. We like our own company, but I think I am going to enjoy a night in a bed instead of under the stars.

Margaret gently pushed her fingers through his mass of blond curly hair and said this is going to be a long job, I don't think this comb has any chance of getting threw this mop, I'm going to have to start at the top and work my way down.

Kevin could feel the niceness of the extra attention he was getting, and he thought, to be honest it felt good; it felt as though he was part of someone else. And as Margaret snipped away at his curly locks and they fell to the ground, Kevin could also feel the warmth of her body as it pressed lightly and sometimes firmly against him. He could smell the clean fragrance of her body, and he could sense that every time they innocently touched, an unknown entity seemed to pass between them. It felt like an extra spark of life, a tiny electric shock that sent a shock wave escaping to the furthest parts his body and once reaching its destination, bounced back to fill his whole body with the feeling of a mass of tingles. He knew he had only ever felt the same sensation twice before. The day he met Janet and the day his son was born. He knew what he believed in, and he knew he was going to have to make a choice, help destiny on its way, or turn away from its help, either way his life would never be the same again.

Margaret broke his thoughts, saying, I'm surprised at mum accepting you so easy and that bit about Gretna Green, I've never seen her so understanding. Just like I said before, Mums always been against me marrying anyone from the village, she used to say she wanted me to broaden my horizons and find someone special from as far away as possible. And that was difficult to do, when the only strangers to come here were normally lost in the first place and probably thought they we better off lost in the second place.

For half an hour Kevin watched his locks fall to the ground, his scalp having lost its mat of insulation started to feel its own tingle as the cooler air moved in.

Chapter Fifteen. The Metamorphosis.

Margaret excused herself and disappeared inside only to return a few seconds later with her father's razor. I'm just going to square off your neck and I'm finished, I've put a clean towel in the bath room for you and you can borrow dads razor to shave your face. Margaret finished Kevin's neck and removed the sheet to allow him to push his own fingers threw what little hair was left. Right get upstairs and get bathed, I've got to help mum get everything ready for tonight.

Kevin smiled and saluting her with his good hand, said, yes sir General Margaret, what ever you say. As he was about to ascend the stairs, he halted and took a quick glance back at his Barbour who was busy sweeping up; he shook his head as he watched her slip one of his locks into her pocket. In the bathroom he turned on the taps and made a small circle with his clothes in the middle of the floor. Placing Bun in the centre to keep her safe while he soaked, it came to him that it had been a long time since his last bath or in fact any creature comforts that went along with a modern home. In the corner of the bathroom stood a full-length oval shaped mirror that returned the reflection of a solid moulded body devoid of fat. It didn't show the signs of deterioration that normally went along with a man whose age had spanned nearly half a centaury, it was more akin to a youth in his early twenties. Looking at his reflection, Kevin thought only of one thing. How stupid his beard looked. He switched off the hot tap and let the cold run until his bath felt safe to get into. He didn't use the bubble bath or even the soap; he just submerged under the water of the huge Victorian cast iron bath and lay there as if dead.

After what seemed an eternity, a red body arose from the hot water and a matching hand reached forward to lift a tall chrome-shaving mirror from the end of the bath, and sat it down on the muscular ripples that were its belly. Splashing water on its steamed up glass, it also revealed the same picture as its bigger brother, so with her father's razor, Kevin started to slowly remove his now unwanted facial hair until the mirrors image showed a once again naked face. When he finally arose from his bath, his Father Christmas image had evaporated to one of an Adonis. Kevin collected his shaven hair from the base of the shaving mirror stand and deposited it in the waist bag that stood beside the oval mirror, then dressed in his original clothes before washing the bath and retiring to his bedroom with Bun.

And that's were Kevin was at seven thirty when the Swan opened to the public, and Margaret went to ask him if he wanted his tea in private or in the bar. She found her bedroom door half open and Kevin lying asleep on top of her bed, with Bun also asleep lying on her side, half inside his shirt, with her head tucked under his chin for safety. Buns nose twitched and her whiskers moved on Kevin's neck, were upon Kevin said its ok I know. Putting his hand on Bun, his eyes opened and his face smiled, its very peaceful here, its not often I put my head on a pillow and fall asleep.

To Margaret, those few words came right out of a wish, good she said I'm pleased. Would you like your tea up here in private, or in the bar?

Up here if it's no trouble.

Ok, be back in five minuets.

At eight fifteen as Margaret and her mum served drinks to a nearly full house, a new man walked down the stairs.

Peggy had to take a second look at this man. Who, dressed in a white silk Chinese outfit, looked twenty years younger than a few hours earlier? Touching her daughter on the arm to attract her attention, nodded towards Kevin, saying a shave and a hair cut and a pair of pyjamas never made your dad look that good.

Oh mum, those aren't pyjamas, they are a traditional Chinese outfit, I've seen them on films, but I know what you mean. He does look rather yummy.

Kevin's loose top was held together at the front with

wooden pegs, much the same as his duffle coat, and also much the same was the pocket were he kept Bun. Bun's nose could be seen twitching in the gap between the second and third peg, and every few seconds the same nose would disappear back inside.

Standing at a gap in the bar, Kevin could feel more eyes on him than those of Peggy and Margaret, but he concentrated on the ones he knew best.

I kept your table free, that's if that's where you want to sit. Margaret found herself also saying, Gosh Kevin you do look handsome, what a difference since this morning.

Peggy gave Margaret a push on the shoulder, saying, before you dissolve on the counter, take Kevin's order and let the man sit down.

Without being asked Kevin said. A half of cider will do when you're ready. And turning he walked away from the bar and up to Joe Semple. Joe still had the blood blister on the end of his nose, though it had, gone a little darker.

What ever Kevin whispered in his ear, no one heard, but Joe must have agreed because he just nodded. The shy side of Kevin would have picked the same little alcove that he sat down in, but tonight was not the night to be shy. His fame had spread, and most of the people their were more interested in him than the band.

Bob Blacklock was the first. Introducing his wife to Kevin, saying, I thought I should have first dibs on you seeing as how we have had tea together.

But his occupation was short lived, on the arrival of Peggy saying I hope you don't mind me fetching your drink but I want to get some work out of her tonight, you understand, don't you. Kevin liked Peggy a lot, she was blunt and to the point, but her words were always said with a hint of joviality. As she wandered away picking empty glasses from the surrounding tables, two pairs of eyes were waiting for her to clear the area. Within a second of her disappearing with the glasses into the kitchen they moved from the bar and sat down on the opposite side of Kevin's table.

Kevin's hand moved over and covered Bun, for before him sat Zorro and Joe Scatter complete with his parrot like terrier on his shoulder, but minus the salmon inside his jacket.

Didn't recognise you this morning, in fact I don't recognise you now. But him that was last here with his wife, old flat foot Blacklock, was saying as how I helped you find those little Clark lasses.

That's right you did, if it hadn't have been for you, it would have taken a lot longer. I may have changed, but you haven't.

I haven't, Joe smiled

Oh you've broadened out a lot, but you are still the same young man I watched poaching salmon in the harbour basin all those years ago.

The word poaching seemed to start off a clockwork action between Zorro and Joe, as first they looked at each other and then over their apposing shoulders and then back to each other, and then back to Kevin. Shush they both said in tandem, then Joe said we don't want everyone to know.

Kevin could have burst out laughing, but instead, kept his composure, the thought of the size of the village and how long Joe had been poaching, if there had been any secrets, Joe's could not have been one of them. Kevin could see they had more on their minds than had said. And inquired, what can I do for you gentlemen.

The clockwork action started again, but once their spring had run down the two men and the terrier lent forward and said together, can anybody do it.

Looking a little lost at their question.

Joe continued, you know, that Gung Fu stuff.

Oh, that, yes I suppose so, I've seen men bigger than you two who could move like a hungry praying mantis.

It's a long time since either of those two were hungry, came a voice from behind them.

Old bat ears, is back, Zorro grumbled.

I heard that to, Peggy said winking at Kevin over their shoulders.

Their clockwork actions didn't work to the sound of Peggy's voice. Instead the two big men just sat still like little children waiting for a school teachers reprimand. When they realised they weren't going to get one, Joe said quietly, would you teach us, I could pay you with salmon.

I could, teach you; in fact I would have loved to. I think it would be most enlightening. My only problem is, I intend moving on, if not tomorrow, then the day after at the latest. If I managed to get away early in the morning, I could be a hundred miles up the road by this time tomorrow.

Unknown to the three, another pair of ears were still listening in on their conversation. Peggy had felt her heart sink, on hearing Kevin's answer, she knew Margaret hadn't expected Kevin to leave so soon, in fact she was sure she was hoping he wouldn't leave at all. Peggy knew it wasn't her place to interfere, but if she had wanted to, her mind was distracted by the arrival of her husband Tom, who said he couldn't sleep and would give them a hand until he felt tired, as he started at four in the morning. Tom was a small man with pointed features and light hair. He had a good sense of humour but would have had to go a long way to beat Peggy's. Tom had been a postman all his life and loved it; it was where he met Peggy. They had, had a hard time, raising two kids, money had always been short, and when they got chance of the Swan, he had decided to stay with the post office just in case anything went wrong. That was twelve years ago, and Tom was still taking no chances. Peggy would say Tom might as well have married the Post Office instead of her. Tom knew Peggy was joking, or at least hoped she was. The top and bottom of the matter, was Tom felt alive when he was on the move, whether walking or driving, it made no difference, he was awake when most people where asleep so he thought he was living twice as long as them. No matter how much he loved her, to him being locked in a pub all day amounted to nothing more than slow death, and anyway, with him not being their, it left room for his pride and joy, his daughter Margaret.

Joe Semple was a better singer than a drinker or a fighter, he and the Renegade's made the night go fast, to fast, for Margaret's liking. No matter how hard she tried to get near Kevin, she found herself either too busy or Kevin already occupied. There was a constant envelope of people around him. There never seemed to be a moment when there wasn't, for as soon as one person left his side, another took up the conversation.

Margaret thought the only way to brake this deadlock was get noticed, so waiting until Joe Semple was in the middle of his third and final set of songs, left the bar and walked up to the him. Margaret waited until the group finished the song they were on, then asked Joe for the mike. She had made up her mind to show Kevin she wasn't just a pretty face. There wasn't much room on the make shift stage even for her slender frame, so Joe decided to give her his space and play his guitar on the floor below her,

Joe rightly classed himself as a professional and was praying that Margaret wasn't going to lay an egg, because it was more difficult to get up on stage and sing a song than most people thought. But he need not have worried because his prayers were answered. for even with all her nerves, Margaret's voice was as strong as his own.

Margaret went into a rock and roll number, and then looking at Kevin carried on with a slow love ballad.

Kevin could feel the depth of conviction in her voice and the look in her eyes told him everything this beautiful young lady was saying. They where words, and feelings, he just didn't need at this time in his life.

As Margaret finished, she bowed to the uproar of applause from the locals and stepped down from the stage to even more applause.

Tom said to Peggy, I don't know why we pay someone else to sing when our lass can sing like that, mind you I never heard her put so much effort into it before, she must be in a good mood with her self.

Peggy knew why, but wondered just how long it would last once her daughter found out how soon the maker of those feelings was leaving.

As Margaret walked from her singing debut, she saw Kevin rise from his seat and walk towards her. Her first thought was that he wanted to dance, but that disappeared quickly as he smiled at her as they passed on the floor.

Kevin looked at Joe, and without words, Joe slipped off his lead guitar and handed it to Kevin, who in turn put the strap over his own head and across his shoulders.

Joe went to the bar and stood next to Margaret, and both said together how does he expect to play it. Even the crowd went quiet as they wondered how a one handed man would try to play a two handed instrument.

The answer came from Bun, a little whisper to her long ears and she produced from her hiding place a leather wrist strap with what looked like a plectrum shaped object protruding out of it. Kevin fitted it to his stump, and then looking up at the crowd took a second to find were his young host was standing. His voice was slow soft and quiet, as he spoke into the mike.

I would like to sing two songs that are close to my heart for the kindness, you have all shown me, I hope you can stand the voice. My first song is for family and friends, long gone but never forgotten.

It's called, I'll Remember You.

He didn't need the mike because the room was in silence. His singing voice had a nasal distortion that gave him a sound all his own, he sang as he spoke, soft and slow, emphasizing every word. The song sounded like a poem but everyone knew it was more a statement of everlasting love. It's hard to pick up the tune that goes with the words without the sound of music, but in this case they will have to be read and not heard.

Chapter Sixteen. The Saddest Song, Of All Time.

Ill always remember you,
just as long, as there is, a summer,
and if the summer goes.
Ill be so lonely,
forever lonely,
because, I'm living only,
too.
Too remember you.

Ill always remember too,
Your voice, as soft as,
as, a warm autumn breeze.
With your sweet laughter,
and the mornings after,
forever after.
Ill, always remember you.

Until, your arms again someday.
I will return to stay.
But until then.
I will, remember, too,
every, bright star,
that we made wishes, upon.
So please Love me always
and promise me always,
that you'll remember too.
That Ill Always Remember You.

L

 Peggy's tearful eyes searched the room for a dry eye, but could find none. So deep was Kevin's conviction, he had captivated the heart and soul of everyone in the building including himself, for his eyes reflected more than the small spotlight that shone on him. Wiping from his cheek the aftermath of his leaking eyes, life began to return to his face, and for a brief second glanced over at Margaret before starting his second song (love you more than I can say). By the end of the song, Margaret had tears of happiness, in eyes of youthful hopefulness, but her mum had different thoughts.

Peggy knew that the first song had said it all. It would take to the end of time, and then some, before Kevin was likely to get over Janet. She knew that there were going to be a lot more tears on the horizon, and from what conversation she had picked up; the horizon wasn't going to be far away. As that, late summer night came to an end, and everyone had exchanged the Swan's hospitality for the warmth of their own beds, Kevin joined Margaret and her mum in the kitchen washing glasses.

I've stacked all the chairs on the tables and if you show me were the vacuum cleaner is, I can give the place the once over.

Peggy could see that he wanted to help, and even though she had her own way of doing things, she wanted him to feel wanted and at home. And if not for his sake then she would make exception for Margaret. As the drone of the vacuum sounded out from the customer's side of the bar, Peggy looked at Margaret and said.

With one hand, I don't suppose he'd be much good at this.

I'll tell you mum I don't think there's anything he couldn't do, and I'm sure Bun would hold these glasses while he washed them.

I'm sure she would, Peggy agreed, but I was wondering, if you've had time for a talk with him to find out what his plans are

O mum, I don't think he's going to stay for long, and I want him to, so much, I know I've only known him a day, but I feel so close to him, its as if I've known him all my life, Its as if he has filled a gap I didn't know I had, but if he goes, he's going to leave me with a gap that no one else can fill, I just know it.

There was a short silence as they stared at each other, then

Margaret continued, is that the way you felt about Dad?

Peggy looked up thinking about her sleeping husband on the other side. Of the ceiling, Yes, I'd have to say we were much the same, probably everyone is, mind you, your Dad and I always did everything together and if we weren't together people would say where's Tom is he sick and vice versa. I've also known people to get married and not love each other, but it cant be much fun, just desperation. Thinking about the words in Kevin's first song, Peggy said, listen love, no matter what your heart is telling you, either take it one step at a time, or ask him straight out, put your cards on the table.

But mum, what will I do if he say's he doesn't feel the same way.

Peggy couldn't say that, that was how she saw the situation, but still thought it better to come out sooner than later, replying. Well that's the chance you take love, but at least you will know where you stand.

If there were to have been any more conversation, time had run out with the dying off of the vacuum, all done, I've never vacuumed floorboards before.

Mother and daughter looked at each other and burst out laughing. Don't mind us lad, Peggy said, we were having such a good chin wag, that I wasn't taking a lot of notice.

Sorry Kevin, Margaret said butting in, our minds were on something more absorbing, we normally just sweep the Bar floor with a brush, never mind.

As the time was after midnight Kevin asked Peggy, would it be to late to go for a short walk with Margaret.

Its not up to me lad, our Margaret's a grown women, and if she says its not to late then its ok with me. Then she added, but thanks for asking all the same.

Outside on the street the night air was warm and still, the old gas lamps dotted sparsely down the pavements on either side of the road gave off a low flickering light, and around each one flew a cloud of kamikaze moths and insects, at least they would have been if they could have got in.

    Kevin said I know where I want to go. So turning left they linked arms and headed towards the cross roads where the big Victorian gas lamp stood in the middle of the road. It also had its little band of followers trying to get into the flame. Kevin was the first to talk, and as usual his voice was slow quiet and full of thought. Looking at the moths he said. Every living thing seems to be heading for a guiding light to commit suicide on.

    Holding his arm tighter Margaret came to a halt and looking up at him said, even you.

    She felt a little kick come from inside him that was nothing to do with Bun. The little kick was a cross between a very short in kept laugh and an equally short in kept sigh.

    Leaning forward he kissed Margaret on her forehead, and before she could return the pleasure, he said, yes, even me. I'm just another moth.

    Turning the corner at the school they headed towards the reading room and the last remaining gas lamp in the village.

    I thought you of all people would have been stronger than a moth.

    Any moth is only as strong as the light that guides it.

    Margaret pulled him to a halt again, and almost aggressive, she spoke sharply. Stop talking in riddles, I know what you mean, I know what you are getting at. Forget about the past, let me, be your light. Please.

    There was no kiss at the end of this pause, and as they carried on walking Kevin started to talk again. I don't normally take the time to explain myself, but the last twenty-four hours has hit me like a bomb blast, it's taken the wind right out of my sales. I see a look in your eyes, I haven't seen in a lot of years. Perhaps its because I just haven't been looking, I don't really know. But there is one thing I do know, you make me feel young again and very, very happy. The trouble is you also make me very, very sad.

    To me, you are physically and mentally a most beautiful young woman.

Margaret stopped him, saying your compliments mean more to me than you might realise, but I hear a but coming.

Kevin replied quickly, you are right, but its not a full but, more a good half one. Running his thumb down her cheek like he had under the old horse chestnut tree, he said, at the right time and place I would have tried my best to keep that lovely smile in the place it belongs. Even in the dim light he could see the sadness on her face. Please don't feel sad he said, but the tell tale signs of a tear trail glistened on her cheek and followed the trail left by his thumb. His words didn't fill her with comfort. Just the opposite. There could have been a time and a place for us, but I think we missed it.

Theirs still plenty of time left Margaret cried as they passed the reading room and headed into the darkness that held the memorial gardens. Sadly and unconvincingly Margaret repeated her words, there's still plenty of time.

Yes you're right love, but what could I give you, my past is a mess. My future will be messier, and, I've got more past behind me than I have future in front of me. I made a promise, and I can't think of any way that I can talk myself out of doing it, not that I want to. The satisfaction I will get, sadly to me will probably be similar to the one I remember when my lad was born. His voice was harder now; any sign of softness was gone. Then instantly it returned to being soft and calm. Today was the first time in ten years that I can honestly say my brain has stopped hurting and the torment in my soul has had some relief. The laughing and singing seemed to take all the bad feelings away, at least for a time. Maybe the laughing hasn't stopped. I just don't know.

That's right, maybe you just needed something to take your mind off your problems, to give you something else to think about.

The simplicity of her answer didn't need the help of any Chinese philosophy to make him understand.

There was a hopeful look on her face that he couldn't see

in the darkness, she carried on talking saying, we can keep you laughing, and keep your mind on the good things in life, and there are good things. Please believe me.

Maybe, you are right, who knows, maybe the laughing hasn't stopped, the only trouble is love when I put my head on a pillow, the night time can be ten times longer than the day time. It doesn't seem to matter how many pillows I add, sleep seems hard to find, I just cannot switch off to the injustices of life.

Well at least you are saying maybe, instead of but, at least that's a start and some were to start from.

I don't know love, perhaps you are right, perhaps it is time to call it a day, but if it is why have I been pushing myself for so long. Kevin looked at her face to face, and all he could see was her dark silhouette. He said frustratingly, talking also with his arms, as he gestured, shaking them up and down. I, have to have justice, I just have to.

Margaret grabbed his flailing arms and held them to her waist. I'm not really a religious person Kevin, but Didn't God say vengeance was his, I think he meant it for everyone. And remember he lost a son as well.

He may have, and I do understand what you are saying. But maybe he knows something I don't, it maybe, he has a softer pillow than me, or maybe he has more than one Wife, more than one Son, and more than one Grandchild.

Maybe he has Kevin, or could it be possible that he is giving you another chance, to have a second wife, a second child, and even a second Grandchild. Isn't it just what you said, Destiny, and being able to spot it when it's given to you? Didn't those words come straight from your lips?

Margaret's thoughts, put into words, were as powerful as any he had heard. They had come from the heart; they were fresh, open and honest. Kevin went quiet, her optimism and fresh outlook had thrown a new light on his life, he fully believed in Destiny, but he had never expected it to call on him before he had full filled his oath. Had he missed the signs, had his tunnel vision on what he wanted to do, clouded what he didn't want to see, if destiny wasn't trying to change his direction why was he standing there wanting a beautiful young lady to carry on holding his wrists tight to her waist. He hadn't noticed, but they had ended up at the memorial gardens main gate. He hadn't a word of contradiction to her hopefulness, and for once his mouth was empty and silent.

They looked at each other and there didn't seem anything else left to do except what comes natural to lips.

The kiss was short, but Margaret felt relief, and free to throw her arms around Kevin's neck. The feeling was good and he knew the bond between them was more than strong. Margaret could feel being held off a little, but realised it was only to stop Bun from getting squashed. In a second she felt herself being picked up bodily, into his arms, and stepping back a couple of paces Kevin sat down between the pillows on the sand stonewall that belonged to the Memorial gardens.

He sat Margaret on his knee and held her around her waist, her grip was still around his neck and by the feel of it she had no intentions of letting go. Their cheeks leant against each other and both could feel the tickle of single unseen tears merging in the darkness. There didn't seem to be words to fit the situation by either party and after a ten-minuet silence reality returned to Kevin. I think we better head back, I've kept you out long enough. I don't want your mum getting worried.

There was no answer from Margaret, not even a reconciled sigh. As long as she could hold onto some part of his body, that was all that seemed to matter.

Letting themselves in the Swam, they found the light in the kitchen the only sign of life. Margaret squeezed the hand she was holding and whispered I'll get us a hot drink, co-co ok.

The replying nod seemed to be said also in a whisper, and as she walked into the kitchen with a head full of thoughts the owner of the squeezed hand lifted two chairs down from their stacked position on a bar table.

Margaret's thoughts, were, what to her felt like a miracle, she had never understood her mum's attitude to local lads or to the one she had for Kevin for that matter, if anything, Kevin should have been the one who was a no-no. But for whatever reason she had, her mum had done a grand job. She had saved her from the village idiots and kept her safe for the total stranger that made her feel like a real complete women.

If Kevin could have read her thoughts he would have told her that miracles had no bearing on the real world. Oh he had real feelings for her, more than he could ever have expected, human nature does that, it's the way it works, human nature had to be one of the strongest forces in the world. Kevin's problem was a stronger force, it was the one called revenge, and he had been practicing it for ten years. Ten years, against one day, was there really a contest.

Margaret didn't want to sleep, but the stress of the day was starting to thump in her head, as she sipped the last of her co-co she found herself thankful to Kevin's statement that it was time for bed They walked up the stairs together and parted with a hug and a kiss. It wasn't what she expected because the hug was Kevin holding her head in his hands and covering her with a line of kisses starting with her nose then continuing every inch up over her head. As he looked down at Buns nose twitching, he smiled and said I only do that for the girls I love, and then he kissed the first two fingers on his left hand and placed them on her lips, now off to bed with you. He stood at his door and watched her tiered feet climb the tight curling wooden carpet less stair to the attic. Within a second he heard her body flop down on creaking springs, then silence fell. She's gone to bed with her clothes on, I suppose it has been a long day, his eyes caught the luminous dial's of her dressing table clock 2.45 am. I suppose to us Bun, time means very little, but this being civilisation, everything evolves around those aluminous pointers and that ticking sound, I suppose that's something else to think about.

Undressing, in the still dark room. Kevin slipped between

the cotton sheets, his naked body jumped at the touch of a Luke warm stone hot water bottle obviously put in by Peggy. Lifting it out he placed it under the bed, and then snuggled under the heavy patchwork over quilt. Bun laid flat out on Kevin's chest, and then pushed forwards with her back legs until she had pushed her head for safety under her whole worlds chin. As Kevin's arm came over her back for support, he said I think we better cut your toenails tomorrow; there was no reply except the inaudible sound of Bun lovingly washing his neck with her tongue.

Pushing the back of his head into the feather filled pillow, he stared at the ceiling. His body was in a different world to his brain and he remembered thinking how fresh the sheets smelt compared to his ex army waterproof sleeping bag, how could something on the inside smell so much nicer than the great outdoors. Wrapping his fingers around Buns back feet he held her closer and tighter to himself. Do you think we have been on the outside to long, and its time to come in? He knew she had heard his whispering sleepy words, by the way her left ear rose and touched his nose, then in even sleepier words he said. Yes, I suppose you are right, and what difference would it make to you, as long as we are together.

Buns head shot out from under Kevin's chin, as an alarm clock in the next room sounded out some ones awakening hour. Kevin looked at the luminous dials of the clock that sat on the dressing table in his room, and they read 4.45 am, they had been asleep two hours. Hearing footsteps descending to the kitchen, Kevin laid a second then decided to follow them. After all, if he had been sleeping on the outside, he would have just about been getting up anyway.

In the kitchen, having a shave was Margaret's Dad. Turning to see who was behind him he said. Oh-hi. sorry if I woke you. The kettles on, make us both a brew, I've got to be in work by 5-15 so I cant stop.

As the kettle started to make steam, Kevin asked, normal is it? Two sugars and one milk.

No, make mine black, and add a bit of cold water. Then turning to face Kevin, he sat down at the table and smiled, saying lovely morning, isn't it. Swallowing down his cold tea, Tom noticed Kevin's hand missing, and said, sorry, if I'd known, I would have mast the tea.

It was Kevin's turn to smile, saying, no problem what so ever.

In less than a minute, Tom had downed his tea saying that's great, he then rose from the chair, and grabbing his lunch box off the sink, continued, saying, lose it in a motor bike accident, I've got a mate done just the same.

Kevin realised Tom had been told nothing, perhaps it was the odd hours he kept. Whatever, he never got a chance to say otherwise as he watched Tom slip out the back door.

As fast as the door closed, it opened again. One milk, how do you pore one milk, over my head that is. Then the door closed again, just as quick.

One hour later, Margaret awoke from a restless, but deep sleep that hadn't been broken by the alarm. Their being no clock in the attic, she didn't know the time, but she had a fare idea it wasn't breakfast time by the tiny amount of light coming threw the open curtains. Her mind was still in a turmoil, and once awake there seemed to be no chance of turning back over, so throwing the covers to the bottom of the bed she got up to find herself fully clothed. What a scruff, she called herself and was about to throw off her clothes and change into fresh ones when she remembered she wasn't in her own room.

Needing some fresh air to clear the cobwebs out of her head, she went to open the window, only to be stopped in her tracks. Was her mind still in a dream? For as she looked down into the walled back garden, she could see, even in the dim light a shadow running up the eight foot walls and doing a back flip when it had reached the top. Then she knew she was dreaming for instead of doing a back flip, it carried on to the top of the wall and ran along the top as though it were a spider or a fly or exactly what it was, a shadow. She couldn't believe what she was seeing, for surly only a shadow could run along the top of an eight foot wall that was covered in broken glass bottles without being cut to shreds. She tried to open the sliding sash windows to get a better look, but they were either stuck with paint or swelled with the early September rain. Now wide awake, she decided to get Kevin's help, and sneaked down the stairs to his room, there was no answer to her gentle knock so she opened the door and not wanting to switch on the light and scare the shadow away, went over to his bed to waken him. The bed was empty, its covers replaced as if not being slept in. Now further down the view from this window was restricted but the shadow was still there.

She knew it could be only one person and now even more so, she didn't want to surprise him and get himself hurt. So taking her time in the dark she went down stairs and out into the yard. The yard door to the garden was closed, and before she opened it, she wanted to wait for noises that would tell her Kevin was on the ground. She didn't have to wait for long before a voice spoke to her from above.

Looking for someone.

Margaret jumped backwards and was about to collide with a stack of crates, when Kevin jumped down and held her. Margaret was nearly out of breath with shock as she babbled out. Are you, all right? Are you not cut to pieces?

Calm down, I'm fine.

But the glass, how did you not cut your feet, I didn't think your shoes could protect you from the pointed bits; her voice faded away to nothing as she looked downward and fainted. When Margaret came around a few minuets later, she found herself lying on the damp grass, her head and shoulders raised up on Kevin's knee. She jumped up to a kneeling position and faced him. Kevin, your feet, you're not even wearing shoes for heavens sake. Why? How? Her mouth was open, but nothing was coming out.

Anticipating her questions, he said it for her. Why are my

feet not cut, because I believe, in myself.

Margaret found her voice again, and in an exasperating tone of confusion blurted out. Cut-Cut, they should be in shreds for heavens sake. What you did was impossible, theirs no person in the world can do what I saw you do without putting themselves in hospital for months, hells bells, they would be lucky if they could ever walk again. No- No Kevin, what you did was impossible.

There is nothing in this world impossible; people walk on red-hot ashes and beds of nails all the time. You just have to believe in yourself. When I was a child, I read a story of a Zulu chief, named SHAKA who made his warriors run threw thorns to toughen up their feet, and even now I get that tingling feeling in my feet, when I think about it. I'm not a religious man, but if the Bible is true, then I think the tingles must be a passed on sensation, to everyone, from Jesus, so that we can all feel a little of what he felt when he got nailed to that cross.

Margaret looked deep in thought and said, It's funny, but I got those tingly feelings in my feet when I saw you walking on the glass, in fact I get them every time I think of something sharp on the souls of my feet, I thought it was just me.

No love, I think every one gets the same feelings, one way or another.

Margaret looked up at Kevin and said I think that SHAKA man must have been a sadist; I'm pleased I didn't work for him.

You are probably right, but, what ever he was, I can see his life story through my eyes, I can read his thoughts, feel his anger and the forces that pushed him. The kid's book I read was just the appetiser, when I was in America; I spent a lot of time researching great people, and what pushed them to success.

When Shaka's name popped up again. I had to find out all I could about him. His story was similar to mine, in the way his family died. But that's really where our stories part company.

He was the illegitimate son of a chief of an African tribe, and because of this his mother and family were frowned upon, and treated like scum. He was once beaten up and left for dead, only to be brought back to life with the loving care of his mother and a strong will to live. All the hatred inside him, seemed to drive him on until one day he matured into a great war Chief, and took over his own tribe. He started to take vengeance on all who had hurt him and his family. And gradually he took over one tribe after another. I always thought that the word Zulu stood for the name of all African natives, just like we are called English. Zulu was Shaka's second name, just like yours is Bryan and mine is Hodgson. SHAKA ZULU ended up ruling a continent one thousand times the size of Great Britain. And every person living in his kingdom bore his second name. They were either, in his family, or they were dead. They were all Zulu's, every last one of them. Can you imagine the power, he held, over all those people? Can you imagine the power you would hold if every one in Great Britain had to have your sir name for their own. It doesn't bare thinking about. Even I couldn't imagine it, never mind him having it one thousand times more. And that's what will power can do for you, if it gets out of hand. Think of all the Great people who have said, not only No, to the word impossible, but yes I can do that, I can make that work, I'm going to find a cure. They all have one thing in common, they believed in themselves. They are so full of confidence it surrounds them like a glove. And as long as there are people out there that believe in themselves and saying there has got to be an answer, then, the world will keep going forwards. You can do anything when you believe, and that is what I've been practising for, for ten years.

  I believe, therefore I can. I've been ready for at least two years, I practice every day so as not to let my adversaries get one day in front of me. The only things that could have stopped me at one time were the creeping up of old age and bad health. Now I've got Bun, my long eared rat to think about and.

  Margaret anticipated what he was going to say and interrupted saying. Me.

  Well that might have been what I was going to say, but

for the love of me, I couldn't live without Bun now, and I wouldn't dare say how much I feel for you, another day like yesterday and I'm going to be closer to you than her.

And you can't let that happen, Margaret said with a resigning smile.

That's just it, I don't know, and I don't think I will until I get away from here.

Margaret frowned, saying, away from here, or me?

Kevin touched her cheek as before and said, a little of the first, but absolutely loads of the second. Even if I go away and didn't want to come back, I still would, just to say hello and keep in touch, that I promise.

That's the second promise you have made to a women, I'll hold you too it no matter what, so don't say it if you think you have any doubts. I'll give you a chance to take it back if you want.

That's the trouble with promises I never give them without a lot of thought, and I've never broken one. That's the other trouble with promises. If you think your mind is mixed up, just think what mine is like. Listen Margaret, there's many a thousand days not broken into yet, and yesterday was only the beginning of today and today the beginning of tomorrow. I have forces pulling me every which way, and I have to follow the force that is pulling me the most. Once I get away, I'll soon know where my heart lie's.

Ok Kevin, I can see for me to try and change your mind at this point in time is wrong, but look after yourself and most of all look after the other lady in your life. Margaret bent over and stroked Bun who was sitting in the middle of the curled up duffle coat and seemed to be doing some digging inside the coat.

Kevin said, go on then, give her it now. Hold your hand out in front of Bun, to make it easier for her. It only took a second for Bun to pick up a metal chain with her mouth and pass it out, dropping it into Margaret's open hand. The chain was made from solid silver, and long enough to go once around a ladies wrist, the two ends were joined by a tiny heart shaped lock no bigger than a farthing, but about four times as fat. An even tinier key, sat in the keyhole of the lock with a spider's web like chain attached to it, and then in turn, it was anchored back to the lock.

Oh it's lovely, but I can't take it Kevin, it must be a family heirloom.

It probably is, but not mine. It belongs more to you than me anyway, and that's for certain. That chain was the present Ada gave me all those years ago as a going away present, it's the only thing I carry with me from my past, except memories. As I said before I think it was the only thing of value see had. I thought there was a good chance she would still be alive and I always wanted to give her it back. Seeing as she's not, we think you should have it, call it destiny if you will, but I'm sure Ada would be pleased.

Margaret picked up the chain and examined it closer in the now lighter but still dark Saturday morning sky. So this was Ada's, what a long circle it's travelled. Looking at both in turn, Margaret said, thank you Kevin, thank you Bun, this really means a lot to me, a real lot. There's probably more to this destiny stuff than we realise.

There is always a lot more to everything, if we humans would only sit down and take the time to absorb the wonders of even the smallest thing. What say we go inside and look at some of the impossible things man has already achieved in the kitchen.

Margaret put the chain in her pocket. And said, would you like some hot buttered toast, and a hot mug of co-co.

Kevin looked at her, and said, I know you didn't realise what you just said, but that was exactly what I meant.

A puzzled Margaret, said, what, hot toast and co-co.

Exactly that. When you go to bed tonight, close your eyes, and think of all the impossibilities that went into the realisation, that ended up being the produce of someone's idea. Those items we all take for granted, like hot buttered toast and hot co-co, they didn't exist before they were an idea.

Chapter Seventeen. Ghosts From The Grave.

As they entered the kitchen, Margaret felt her heart drop as she noticed for the first time Kevin's duffle bag leaning against the table leg. She knew now, their time together was even more limited than she had first thought. It was harder for her to hold the smile on her face, than the weight of the slices of bread, but managed to keep it by jokingly saying, sit down, while I make us some impossibilities.

Time always seems to go faster the shorter it gets. And for the, now, not so odd couple theirs was no exception. There were so many things to say, yet so little could be said under the circumstances. Until, of coarse, his final ones.

Its time we were on our way.

Mum won't be long, until she's down, are you not going to wait and say goodbye. She'll be upset if she misses you.

I have to go now love; I think your mum wants me to stay just as much as you, but don't worry she'll understand. I can find my own way to the front door; you stay here and keep the kettle boiling for Peggy. Pushing his chair back, Kevin stood up, but a now trembling Margaret quickly followed him. He wanted to tell her to sit down again, but just hadn't the heart. Stepping towards each other, Kevin said, I was told in deaf and dumb language that when a man does this to a women, it meant he loved her, and in saying so, his left hand came up, and he ran his thumb down her cheek.

Margaret felt a tingle go through her body as she remembered all the other times he had done the same to her. And that was before she had even had feelings for him, truly now she knew that their feelings went both ways.

A happy and sad tear collided with Kevin's thumb, prompting him to Place the tear moist thumb to his lips and taste the salts of her emotion. Leaning forward, Kevin kissed her first on the nose and then on her forehead, and then picking up his bag, he threw it over his shoulder.

As their eyes never parted, Margaret knew he was hurting in all the same places as she, and even though they were both voiceless, she found the energy to whisper as he turned and walked away. Please don't forget me!!

As she heard the Swans front door close, there was part of her wished he had heard and part of her didn't, destiny would be the only one to know if he did. The kettle for her mum forgot about, she flopped lifeless into her chair and was about to rest her head in her arms on the tabletop, when she remembered the chain and fumbled gently in her pocket to retrieve it.

Outside, Kevin was heading for Yukkies brow under the watchful eye of Bob Blacklock and P C Shaw. Bob had been sweeping the pavement in front of his shop when an off duty John Shaw who lived in the police house above with his wife Sheila, joined him while taking his black Labrador for an early morning walk. Their little chat, interrupted by the lone man heading out of the village the way he had come in, John was the first to speak. Do you think he'll be back?

Bob didn't need time to think of an answer, he knew it already. That, my friend, will all depend on the rabbit and how long it lives. For my guess is, the longer it lives, the longer Hodgson keeps out of trouble.

How do you work that out Bob?

Well, I think that the only reason he hasn't finished the job he came back to do, is because he would be the most likely suspect, and he doesn't know what would happen to the rabbit if he were jailed.

I see, that does make sense, and if the rabbit died he would only have himself to worry about, and he doesn't worry one bit about himself. So he would just go and do the job and face the consequences later.

Exactly Bob replied, there's no doubt about it, not in my mind anyway, I'd bet money on it.

If you would bet money on it, you must be a hundred and ten percent positive. do you think we will hear from him again.

From him or about him, one way or another, Kevin Hodgson has been newspaper material for a lot of years, and I don't think it will stop now. As the Americans would say the Lone Ranger Rides again, and I think the best is still to come, mark my words.

Ye Bob but the sad thing is Hodgson doesn't have Tonto or silver bullets to help him.

Oh yes he has John, he has something far better than them; at least for now anyway, he's got the Rabbit.

.As Kevin walked out of sight, and the world of the two men, their ears met with the sound of Tom Bryan and his red Morris minor post office van. Morning Tom, both men greeted, as he stepped out and opened the public post box that was sunk in the wall with a bunch of keys that weighed more than him.

Great morning isn't it lads. Ay, look at this, them kids have been stuffing apple scrunt's in my letterbox, where's a policeman when you need one.

John didn't rise to the bate, he had more than once been wound up by Tom's joking remarks, instead he just said, I see your lodgers moved on.

Closing the metal door, so it would awaken the dead. Tom Said, ye I saw him getting into, Father Eric's van, he's probably hitched a lift to town. Come on Bob, lets get inside and see what you've got for me, I cant stand talking here all day. Then looking at John, Tom said, and you, watch my van, I don't want it filled with apple scrunt's when I come back out. Laughing, the little man herded the giant shape of Bob, back into his post office, saying loud enough for anyone to hear as he closed the door behind himself. They are never around when you need them.

Smiling, Bob shook his head and said. One of these days Tom, them two young PCs are going to get you back for winding them up all the time, mark my words, they have probably got you already booked for six months holiday in strange ways.

Bob's, few words of wisdom, put Tom in an even more

jovial frame of mind, Cant do that he said, I'm an out standing citizen, a pillar box of the community. This village, would come to a stop, without me, I keep the place going.

Ye, you do that Tom, along with those two lads.

In the Swan, Peggy had arrived down stairs to join in her daughter's misery. The kitchen was unnoticed by Margaret, filling up with steam, as she fondled Kevin's gift.

Switching off the kettle, Peggy said, I take it he's gone. As Margaret just sat in silence looking at her hands on the table Peggy continued, kettle's well boiled, do you want a cuppa strong tea.

I, just want him back mum, I just want him back.

I'll make you one anyway love, she said, knowing that only time or another man could help a broken heart, and knowing her daughter as she did, the second option wouldn't even get a look in. The tea, brewed, and pored into mugs, she sat down next to her. It'll work out ok In the long run love, just wait and see, here take a drink of this. Peggy handed Margaret the mug of tea and in doing so noticed something in her daughters other hand. What you got their love.

Only taking in half, of what her mother had said, Margaret looked at her mum and said, what was that, then quickly woke up, saying, sorry mum, I was miles away, it's a going away present from Kevin.

Drink your tea love and give us a look, it looks nice, if not expensive.

Margaret took a sip of her tea, and handed her mum the chain.

With only a second's examination, Peggy dropped it on the table as though it were hotter than the tea they were drinking. Peggy's face drained of colour, as she said over and over, Oh My God, Oh My God.

What's wrong mum, you look like you've seen a ghost.

A very shaken Peggy, said, I have love, this chain looks just like the one, my grandfather gave my Mum for her twenty first birthday. It was handed down to Ada when Mum died, and when she died; we searched her cottage from top to bottom and couldn't find it.

That's right Mum, I remember you telling me that Ada didn't have a penny to her name when you emptied her house after she died. Kevin said he thought it was the only thing of value she had, and always wanted to return it. He wrote to her a few times, but never got a reply, and thought she had moved.

I don't understand love, how did Kevin come to have it, if it is the same one my Mum had. If it was Mum's, I couldn't see even Ada selling it.

She didn't sell it Mum; she gave it to Kevin as a present, for getting him so drunk on her elderflower wine, that he ended up having to stay the night. He said he was legless, and I suppose it wouldn't have looked good for him, being a police cadet, and going back to his digs in that state. Especially since he was supposed to be looking for the bodies of those little Clark girls.

Peggy seemed to go into a world of her own, her mind was in a state of total confusion. She kept repeating over and over, He stayed the night. He stayed the night.

Margaret could see her Mum was feeling worse than her, what's wrong Mum, I've never seen you like this.

Peggy looked at the clock, then Margaret, then the chain. I need your Dad; her voice was one of total panic. Go and phone Bob and see if he's left the post office yet, Hurry love.

Margaret said. Mum, if the chain means so much to you, what's the problem you can have it back now. I'm sure Kevin wont mind.

Just phone your Dad, and tell him to drop everything. The tone of her voice meant no arguments.

Margaret knew something was more than wrong. Her Mum made all the decisions, her dad was always pleased to agree, that's the way it was, and always had been. Why now did she need his help? It would have been quicker to run across to the post office, but her Mum said phone.

Picking up the phone in the bar, Margaret dialled the number for the post office. And shouted, its ringing mum.

Peggy could hear her daughters half of the conversation.

Bob, has Dad arrived yet, he has, and he's still their, no I don't need to talk to him, just tell him to come home right away, yes right now, this minute, tell him to hurry.

Within the time it took, to hang up the phone, Tom was outside the Swan.

Margaret opened the front door to her Dad, who was in a second asking in earnest, what was wrong.

I don't know Dad, but Mum's really upset, I've never seen her like it before, quick she's in the kitchen.

Tom rushed past his daughter shouting Peggy, Peggy love, what's wrong?

Closing the front door, Margaret followed her Dad into the kitchen and found her Mum and Dad standing with their arms around each other, and her Dad saying come on love, calm down and tell me what's wrong.

Its happened Tom, it's finally happened.

What has happened love, I don't understand. What, has finally happened.

On the table, Tom, look what's on the table. Ada gave it to Kevin and he's had it all this time.

Tom turned, and his eyes focused on the tiny chain. He seemed to grasp most of the situation without any more prompting. Asked, are you sure that's it?

Yes love, I'm as sure as I can be.

Tom put his hands on Peggy shoulders, and squeezed. What do you want to do love, I take it you've said nowt. Reading Peggy's pleading eyes he let out a big sigh, and motioned Peggy to sit down. For once in his life it was his turn to take charge. Turning to his daughter, he said, come and sit down as well love; I can see this is going to be a bad day.

Sitting around the table, Margaret was at a loss to the situation but said nothing. Her Dad looked at her, then back at her

Mum. Sighing again, he said, why don't you check that its still their, then at least we'll know it's the right one.

Tom, it probably got lost years ago, but it doesn't matter, I just know, it's the same one.

Lets look anyway. Shall we.

Peggy's hands were trembling, as she picked up the chain, and holding the tiny lock between the thumb and forefinger of her left hand she pulled the tiny key out of the key hole with the opposite thumb and forefinger. Turning the lock around the opposite way, Peggy exposed a half sized keyhole that fitted only the first half of the tiny keys teeth. Putting the key, in the hole, she turned it slowly. Before it had made one complete turn, the back of the lock popped open. Turning the open back, to face, first her husband, and then her daughter. Peggy said, with a still shaking voice, that lady's your grandma.

Relieving her Mum of the lock, Margaret said quietly, as she looked at a tiny black and white photo of a young ladies head and shoulders, this is my Grandma. I didn't know there were any pictures of her.

That's the only one love. She was fourteen when that was taken, see her hair, it looks just like yours, in fact if you look at your school photos, she resembled you a lot.

Mum I'm mixed up; I don't see this as being a tragedy.

It is love, and I'm sorry we haven't told you before, but you have to know now, because now we know were the chain has been all this time.

Tom reached out and held his daughters hand. What your Mum is trying to say is that, Tom could say no more. His voice just dried up.

Come on Dad spit it out.

Tom licked his lips and picking up Peggy's mug and swallowed a giant size swallow of tea. Ok love, but this isn't going to be good, and there's no easy way of saying it. With tears flooding down his face, he blurted out. When your Grandmother died, this chain was her only valuable possession, and as tradition demanded, it was handed down to the eldest child. In this case, it was Peggy's sister Ada.

Margaret gripped Tom's hand tight, and said, Ada, was Mums sister.

Tom returned Margaret's grip, and said. Yes love, but the truth of the matter is, Ada, wasn't just your auntie, she was your, real Mum.

For a second Margaret was spellbound, and then blurted out, as realities hit her. But she can't be, she died before I was born, and if she had been then that would mean you couldn't be my Mum and Dad.

Tom looked Margaret in the face, his eyes were still full, and trying not to let them overflow anymore, he said. The truth of the matter is love, Ada died shortly after you were born. We didn't see a lot of her in those days, if any at all. We didn't even know that she was pregnant, and only found out when we went on one of our six monthly visits. The second we walked through the door, we could see that being nine months pregnant wasn't the only thing wrong with her. I ran all the way for old Doc Robinson. But by the time we got back, you had been born, and Ada had haemorrhaged and no matter what old Doc Robinson did, he couldn't stop the blood, and Ada died. In those days it was easy kept quiet. We lived out in the wilds, and no one saw much of us, so every one took it for granted you were ours. Old Doc Robinson signed your birth certificate as us being your parents, so it was easy. Ada told us she had letters from the father that she kept in a secret place, but we couldn't find it, we searched the cottage from top to bottom.

I think I know were that place is Margaret said, her voice worse than Peggy's, then taking in the situation said, but I'm not bothered. Well I am. But I'll never think of you as anything but my Mum and Dad.

We think we understand love, this has got to have been a hell of a shock, and we feel so guilty having kept it from you all this time. We have always loved you like a daughter, and we always will.

    Look Mum, Dad. I'll say it again, as far as I will ever be concerned, you two will always be my real Mum and Dad. And no one will ever need to know different, nothing is going to change, we are still a family.

    Peggy spoke up. That isn't the problem love. We now know who your real Dad is, and that's the worst part of this whole situation. Ada told us just before she died, that she gave your Grandma's chain to the father as a going away present.

    Margaret went quiet for a second, thinking things over. Then stood up letting go of Tom's hand as it finally hit her, and she cried out. Kevin is my real Dad. She sat down, as quick as she had stood up, and even though her mouth was open, she could say nothing more.

    Peggy said, I'm so sorry love, but that's the way it looks to us as well, the irony of it is that I've spent all these years trying to protect you from marrying your half brother because I thought your farther came from this village, and all the time I was wasting my time, and yours. Peggy stood up and said. I need something stronger to drink. Then looking back at Margaret said. It isn't any wonder you felt so much for each other, who could have guessed any of this was going to happen, and now he's gone.

    Aw Mum, I forgot about Kevin. I've got to catch up to him and stop him. This is probably the one and only thing that would stop him from taking on those three men, and ending up in jail.

    I don't think, there's any chance of catching him now, I saw him getting a lift with Father Eric half an hour ago, he could be anywhere by now.

    And what if we have got it wrong, we would look right Wally's then. Peggy said returning from the bar with three stiff drinks. Those letters Ada told us about would prove everything. But they were well gone when we looked for them, never mind thirty odd years later.

    Listen Dad, I told you before, I think I might know were

they are, that's if no one else has found them. Come on, take us up to Ada's cottage, I'm not going to settle till I've looked for them and know for sure.

Peggy and Margaret climbed into the back of Tom's post office van via the seat less passenger side door. Pushing the mail to one side Peggy gripped the steel mesh for balance behind the drivers seat and Margaret did the same, only she shuffled her feet into the space were the passenger seat had been removed.

Tom turned the ignition key clockwise and the ignition light came on, then pulling the little black starter button to the left of the key, the engine burst into life, and they were off. It only took a few minuets for the trio to reach Ada's lifeless cottage and the van had hardly come to a stand still before Margaret had the van door open. Margaret was the first inside the cottage and Peggy and Tom found her in the living room staring at the alcoves on either side of the chimneybreast.

Tom asked, what are we looking for love?

Margaret replied. Kevin said that Ada kept all her valuables in a small tin, that she kept hidden behind a loose brick in the cupboard on the side of the fire, but he didn't say which one.

Green mould had covered the walls, due to the years of damp. But it still didn't take long for Tom to find a loose brick once he knew what he was looking for. Pulling it out with both hands, Tom lost his grip on the slippery brick and it dropped to the floor. But before it had made a thud, Margaret's hand was in the hole and pulling out its generations of secret contents. The picture on Ada's favourite tin had been lost in the rusts of time but the box was still solid.

Open it out side, Peggy said, we wont be able to see anything in here.

Even after all their sadness, and the shocking revelations of the morning, all three felt a child like excitement that was felt on Christmas morning. Perhaps the Father Christmas figure of Kevin had brought Christmas early to three people in

Hayborough this year. Outside in the light, Margaret sat on the wall were she had sat with Kevin the day before. With the tin on her lap, Tom held the bottom while she got her finger nails under the lid and pulled. The lid popped open to reveal a 1933-penny, a puppy's first tooth, a little bag of mixed dried seeds and three letters. Two were from Kevin to Ada, and the other was addressed to Kevin, but marked in big letters. GONE AWAY, RETURN TO SENDER. Taking out the contents of the dry but much faded letter, Margaret found Ada's printing, difficult to read. Some of it was because she was discussing their one night of friendship, and the other was Ada's lack of schooling.

What does it say love, Peggy asked. Go on read it out aloud.

Margaret said it wont is easy, but I'll try.

Dear Kevin

I hope you don't mind me sending you this letter, but you have written me two letters and I was hoping you were interested in me. If you are not, please don't stop writing because no one else writes me letters, and I have something to tell you that I don't know that you will be to pleased about. I hope you can read my spelling because I didn't go to school and I have no one to help me. Not that I want any one else to know my business anyway. I know your address is right because I copied it off your letters. Please don't let someone else read what I am telling you, and please don't be mad when I tell you that when you stayed the night because of the drink I gave you. I was a wife to you when you were asleep. I have never been a wife to a man before you and now I know I have done bad because I have felt ill and been much sick when I wake up in the morning. I was hoping you haven't been sick also, but if you have, you will now know I caused it by being a wife to you. If you don't write back I will know you are mad at me giving you the sickness, but I wont be mad at you ever, because it was my fault. I will always be here and your friend. Lots of thinks. Ada.

Oh Mum she was having morning sickness, with me, and didn't even know it.

I'm not surprised love, in my day no one told us about the birds and bee's. We were kinder left to find out on our own, it wasn't until we got what Ada was describing, that made us go to the Doctors and he would tell us we were going to have a baby. It may sound stupid, but when I look back now to when you were born, I don't think Ada knew that she was having a baby until you arrived, and in turn, realised Kevin was the Dad. We just took it for granted, she knew all along. It may sound even more stupid, but she may not even have known what caused you in the first place.

Mum we have to catch up with Kevin he has to know.

Tom hadn't said a lot, because the conversation up to now had really all been ladies talk, and as he had also been brought up in an age where men found it embarrassing to talk openly, even to their wives about ladies problems, he had kept quiet. But it was now time, as he saw it, to take charge.

It depends were Eric dropped him off. Lets get back and I'll phone in sick or something, then I'll borrow our Billy's car, find Eric, and then find Kevin.

Margaret put the letters back in the tin, and they all clambered into the little red post office van and reversing out onto the moor road, they headed home. Arriving at the Swan, their luck was in, for Father Eric was just pulling up on the other side. Margaret was about to jump out, and run across the road with a mouthful of questions, but Tom stopped her.

Listen love, I ain't ashamed about nothing we've done, now or in the past, but just like Ada, I don't really want everyone knowing our business, not just right now, anyway, so would you mind if I had a talk with Father Eric.

Margaret, was impatient, and wanted to rush over herself, but Peggy held her back by the shoulders saying, I think your Dads right.

Tom opened the van door and walked across the road

just as Father Eric was leaning his ladder up to a bedroom window.

Morning Tom, Father Eric called out, I was going to have a early start to make up for yesterday, but I forgot my ladder, and had to go all the way home again.

Yes, I saw you giving our lodger a lift this morning and I was wondering where you dropped him off at.

Not paid his bill has he, Father Eric joked.

No, nothing like that, it's just he left something behind and we thought he better know before he got to far away.

Oh I see. Well if it's any help, I dropped him off at the shore cross roads. He didn't say much, but I kinder gathered from what he did say, that he was heading home in a roundabout way. Mind you he did say he was coming back no matter what.

Tom said thanks, and was about to turn away, when a thought hit him. Can I borrow your van, to catch up with him? It would save us a lot of time; it's worth a few pints on the house.

Thanks for the offer Tom, but you would be wasting your time. On my way back, I saw him get a lift in an open top, E type Jag sports car, they were heading towards Carlisle, and Tom, for a few pints, you can borrow my van anytime, without asking. But this old tub couldn't catch up with that sports car, even if the roof rack had wings, he'll be twenty miles away by now, best just keep his stuff till he comes back.

Tom smiled, trying not to show his pain, he turned and started to walk away. Within one stride, he stopped and looked back, saying , sorry Eric I'm forgetting my manners, there'll be a pint on the bar for you anyway.

Back at the post office van, Tom told Margaret and Peggy what he had been told. Looks like we either wait until Kevin returns on his own or in the mean time I'll ask the post office to find out where he lived, in fact Bob should be able to tell us that. I'll take some time off work, and looking at Margaret he said, your Mum can look after the Swan while you and I go looking for him, maybe tomorrow or the day after. But in any case, just as soon as I can find where he lived and arrange to borrow a car. What do you say?

Margaret was a realist and knew what her Dad was suggesting, made sense. Thanks Dad, that'll do fine. As the three walked threw the Swans front door. Margaret said to Tom. Did you ever, want to kiss a rabbit, Dad?

No, love, your Mum was always a little on the jealous side. It would have been bad enough for me, but even more unhealthy for the rabbit. Your Mum would have cooked it and made me eat it.

A little smile lit up her face. She thought for a second as she stood in the doorway, holding onto the latch. Then said, Dad, Did you ever talk to a tree.

Tom had no idea, the reason behind her strange questions, but gave her as straight an answer as he could. I never had any reason to; besides, a tree never spoke to me.

Closing the front door behind them, Margaret said, do you think you would know if one did?

THE END

Author's After-word and dedications

I once saw a film about the life of the man who wrote Tom Thumb, and many other mythical people. I think it was one of the brothers Grimm. As he lay on his bed dieing, all the imaginary people inside his head came and sat by his bedside and pleaded with him not to die. When he asked them why they were bothered, they replied, if he died before he wrote the stories about them, then they would never be born and no one would ever know about them, needless to say the little people's pleadings gave him the will to fight his illness and bring his dreams into reality. The Death of my Father, made me realise, that time for myself was getting shorter, and if I wanted to put my dreams into reality, I had better get on with them. In my following two novels I want to bring to life all the imaginary people inside my head. Not only do I want to I bring them to life but also I hope to prove their existence. The Promise is mostly fiction, but the people are real and mostly still alive as this book goes to the publishers. I would like to thank everyone for their kind permission in being allowed to use their names and I hope this book gives them the fifteen minuets of fame they justly deserve. I think my Father would have been totally overwhelmed by the amount of attention he received when he died. Between the local and national press, the television coverage, the amount of people and friends that came to his funeral and his annual memorial rugby league match between Elbra Rangers and Egremont, I am sure he would have been overwhelmed. My Fathers whole life of seventy four years had been a labour of love for Elbra Rugby club and Brookland Rovers, and I don't think he ever did anything that he didn't want to, and apart for my mother getting hurt, I don't think he would have seen his own death as a tragedy. To him, a tragedy would have been the loss of a young life, like the four young men, who along with my father I now want to dedicate this book too.

Anytime I have seen a dedication, it normally says, this book is dedicated to Joe Bloggs or who ever, and that is all.

In this instance I would like to say a little more.

Keith (Cow Hee'd or Stewy) Stewartson.

Keith died of a terminal illness, and his nickname though not very flattering was not meant in anyway a degradation to his looks but it did suit his build. The youngest of three brothers, he stood about five foot nine and was a stocky big boned lad who played professional rugby league. Keith, for all his size, was not an aggressive person, a few inches taller and he would have been unstoppable, even so, when you saw him running towards you with a rugby ball, held against his chest, playing Russian roulette, would have seemed a more safer pastime. I've spent many a good night in Maryport Rugby Club, being entertained by Keith donning his role as a stand up comic. He never showed any sign of nerves or stress, he would just jump up on a chair and start his act as though it were as normal as drinking a pint. One afternoon, after finishing a rugby match. I remember getting changed in our Maryport changing rooms, when a little boy of about five years of age, with straight shoulder length blond hair shouted out, I love you daddy. Keith replied I love you, too, son, and when the cheering died down, he put his hand on his heart, and said, doesn't he, just get you right here. Sometime prior to mid 1985, in my roll as Allerdale Dog Warden, I had put in a charge for a straying dog that belonged to Keith's Dad, on meeting Keith, on Ewanrigg road some days later, he told me, he was disappointed in me and didn't think I had it in me. Keith never got angry or aggressive, cheeky or swore. He just wanted to give me his opinion in a gentlemanly way, he didn't even fall out with me. He was, what he said, just disappointed in me. I think Keith's version of friendship meant that he just couldn't understand why I did it. To Keith, you never did, even a distant friend a bad turn. A friend was a friend no matter what.

George (Poggy) Fiddler

George also was a professional rugby player, and died of a terminal illness. I have known a few people die this way, and all I can say is, they must be the bravest people on this earth. George was a similar build to Keith, but was shapelier and had super star looks. Keith used brute strength to power his way through the opposition, were as George had that extra turn of speed and jinkyness to side step, and run around the opposing players. Just like Keith, George also had loads of brothers and sisters, and both families, were, what I would call, uncomplicated, none problem people, the kind you like to live next door to. To one little lad, George was nearly as popular as the Beatles, and when he went to the hairdressers, and asked for a George Fiddler hair cut. The trouble was the hairdresser had never heard of George. I've known George's family, for thirty years, and I worked with George when he first left school. He was a happy lad, but I found him, not only easygoing, but also very stubborn. We worked together, modernising houses. There was a tradesman, a labourer, (me) and there was the apprentice (George). We were on peace work, which meant, every job had a price, and once we completed it, we got the money. The tradesman got what he did, and I got, what I did. The fly in the ointment was we both shared the profits, of any work George finished. Because George was the apprentice the law stated, he was on a static basic wage and no more, and couldn't collect any extra money for the work he did. George thought it an unfair law, and also unfair that we collected for the work he did. So he told us he was going to down tools, once he had reached his basic wage. And he was right; we would have grumbled ourselves if someone else had been getting money we had worked for. It ended up that the only way we could do it was give him the money out of our wages, once we got it.

I knew George was ill, but I had also heard he was getting better, so I didn't push myself to see him, and my regret is, I never got to see him before he died. Time went fast for me, but even faster for George.

Billy (Bull) Turnbull.

Billy lived just around the corner from me, and I must have known him from an infant. He was one of those happy go lucky lads that everyone liked. You couldn't have fallen out with him if you wanted to; he had a permanent smile, and even talked with a chuckle in his voice. I don't know if he got the nickname Bull, from his sir name or his size, he was always three inches taller than me, and about two stone heavier. Billy didn't come from a big family; he just had one sister, called Sheila.

Billy died from a road traffic accident. And I went to his funeral, along with hundreds of others, it seemed like the whole town was there. Back in the nineteen sixties we all knew girls were the opposite sex, but that was about it. There wasn't many of us with any first hand knowledge, and that included Billy. Billy was about the tallest lad in our gang, but he was always the shyest and the one least likely to get into bother, he never got into any fights and I can't remember him dating any girls until his late teens. When he did start dating, the girls he wet out with, were always beautiful, the ones that took your breath away, and only the bravest would have dared ask for a date. For a lad so shy, I never knew how he did it, they must have asked him for a date, and probably had to stun him with a tranquilliser dart to stop him running away. Of the four lads I am dedicating this book too, I have known Billy the longest, but I have probably the least to say about him, because I never knew him do anything wrong and I don't think anyone else ever did. He was a big quiet lad, that talked, and laughed the whole time, he got on with everyone, it didn't matter who they were. I can't remember Billy ever saying a bad thing about anyone, and how many people can you say that about.

Big John Casson.

John was the opposite, in most respects too Billy, I don't think John could ever have be called shy. Full of confidence John Casson was probably born a ladies man, he was about four inches taller than Billy, leanly muscled, dark straight hair with a quiff. He was just like the words in that old song, (Big Bad John). They go, (he was broad at the shoulder and narrow in the hip, and everyone knew, you didn't give no lip, to big John) I first knew of him, when I was old enough to go to the Maryport Palace Ball Room, probably around 1965 at the old age of 15. In those days, Friday nights at the Palace was the in thing, all the lads strutted around the edge of the dance floor trying to look, cool, mean, and indestructible. That was, until they caught the eye, of one of the two bouncers, where upon, coolness, meanness and indestructibility went out the window, at least until they got out of ear shot, and the coolness came back with the words. (Who, do they think they were looking at)? Johns, main friend, Dick Newton, was the second bouncer. These two men were Maryports answer to Frank and Jessie James or Butch Cassidy and the Sundance Kid, not that they went around robbing trains, they didn't. But, they where, real, men, in the eyes of the younger generation, who, just as today, all wanted to imitate their heroes. I cant remember John, ever dancing, but I do remember Dick doing a touch of Elvis, holding his arms out in front of him, with his fingers, pointing, to the floor, with the coolest of grins on his face, all done to the music, provided by Joe Semple and the Renegades. Only in real life, they were a five-piece group, and Joe and the lads never acted as in my story, though Joe's grandson did say his granddad still likes a pint on the odd occasion. I met John, when my Dad bought a fishing boat and renamed it The Vital Spark. John, myself, and Billy Bryan (a real life cousin, and nephew, to Margaret and her real life Mum and Dad, Peggy and Tom) would go hand hauling a six fathom net, and more than once, had to get rescued, from the Solway, with the net in the propeller, etc, etc, etc.

Today there's a law against everything, but in the sixties and early seventies, things were a lot different and easier going, and we still knew how to laugh. We used to drive around Maryport's two docks, in my mini car that had no floor. Bouncing through the water filled potholes, the water would splash up covering John, who never did anything but roar with laughter. We spent a lot of time together either fishing or working on the docks, were sometimes John would send me alone to the shop, (possibly to save himself another wetting) for his crunchy bars and cream soda, or maybe his hallowed Golden Virginia.

Dropping John off at his back garden gate, we saw Johns wife Margaret hanging out the washing, wearing a head scarf to cover the curling rollers she had in her hair. John spoke out without a second's thought, (look at that, she's got her curlers in, and I haven't told her, she can go out yet). He had that same smile on his face, as if joking, but I never knew whether he was serious or not, and you have to remember, this was the early 1970's and not all, but most women still took their roll as a serviant house wife. Not many days later, a few of us were working on the far dock gates nearest the sea. We were trying to close them after years of un-use, and this was being done by a manual monkey winch, a lorry pulling, and the gates own six man hand operated winch. The tide turned and started to refill the dock, and the sea's own weight was now pushing the gates open, making it impossible for us to continue, so we placed the coil of rope that we were using as a winch brake, over the removable handle we were using and then in turn over the lower handle stub, thus jamming it, when our handle took up the slack. A few minuets before this took place, destiny, if that's what you can call it, took a hand. John who was wearing my woolly hat, swapped places with me, because he said, he could get a better push, on the outside. Within a few minuets every aid we were using, was uncoupled except the rope, which was there to stay. As we walked away from the winch, a farmer friend, of the man in charge, asked John, to put another knot in the already knotted loose ends of the rope. As John did so, maybe, because of the extra pressure from the incoming tide, the rope came off, releasing the winch handle which hit John on the back of his head killing him instantly. As he lay motionless on his back, he looked perfect, except for the massive blood loss coming from his unseen wound.

From the age of eleven, I had worked with a local vet, helping out on every kind of operation, and I knew, that even if we had, had, a hundred surgeons right there, there was nothing anyone could have done. P C John Shaw was watching with my father, on the other side of the dock, and it was he that was nominated to go and tell Johns wife Margaret. Before this happened, Margaret had already been taken into hospital with a miscarriage still not knowing John had died, I would not have wanted John Shaw's job, and lucky for him his orders were given to another officer to be carried out.

At the time, I believed, because we had exchanged places, John had been killed in my place, and I took it real bad, I thought it was my fault. Then about a week later, I had a dream while asleep in bed. I was looking into a room, were John was lying dead on the top of a bed, with Margaret either sitting or kneeling at the far side of the bed, her hands held out, as if holding him. Leaving a perfect image behind himself, he rose and came to the door. He smiled at me, and said, don't worry Barrie, everything's, all right, he then closed the door. When I awoke, I would have said it was just a dream, brought on through worry, except, that I felt as though a Great weight had been lifted from my shoulders. The dream and the feelings are still with me and still as strong today. When my Dad died, my Mother asked me to take anything I wanted that was his, and also did I want John Casson's tobacco tin. My Mother opened it and said look it still has the tobacco and papers in it. I couldn't believe, what I was seeing, my Dad had never said he had it. To me it was like finding the Holy Grail. I put it in a bag, with some of my Dads clothes and took it back to

Stranraer were I live. The next day, I hung the clothes in the wardrobe, and was about to put John's very worn Golden Virginia tin in a safe place, when I decided to see if the tobacco still held its scent after 30 years. To my disbelief, the tin was empty, it hadn't been opened, their wasn't any tobacco or papers left in the bag or spilled on the clothes. I rang my Mother, and asked her if I had been dreaming, did she, or did she not, open the tin and show me the contents. She told me, she did, and I wasn't dreaming. Because of John Casson, I now look at life or death from a different angle, never a final one. When my Dad died, my Mother said, why couldn't he have had ten more years, my answer is this. Every thing has to be looked at from a different angle, as a child my Mother told me the story of my Dads El-Amain Scars. These were scars on his belly; he got in the Second World War that made him look as though he had six belly buttons. The story goes, that after having most of his stomach removed, He wasn't expected to live, and therefore my Mum and Dad were going to get married in hospital, before he died. Because of the same, the hospital let in two drunken men to say their good-bys, but they got my Dad laughing and he made a recovery, and lived on to the age of seventy-four.

    The way I look at it is this, someone had already given my Dad over fifty extra happy years of life with my Mother, forty odd more, than the ten, my Mother so desperately asked for. Perhaps my Mothers prayers were answered the first time, and she just didn't get the chance to ask the second time.

    I hope I haven't offended anyone with my description of their Brother, Son, Father or friend, I' only told it as I saw it. People closer to them, would have known them much better. But, how ever sad, I am sure the lads would want us to keep on laughing, because laughing helps keep you young and healthy.

                                              B W Bryce
                                              January 11th   2002
                                              Stranraer